It started with two beautiful girls.

Napoleon Solo met Denise Fairmount in Paris, and that night in his hotel suite they were attacked by an eerie barrage of killing sound. . . .

He met copper-haired Jerry Terry in a plane going to Germany, and before long they were shot down. . . .

Then he met the twisted genius Golgotha, whose face was a skull-like travesty of hideously scarred tissue, and he learned of the endless variety of horror.

U.N.C.L.E.

THE MAN FROM U.N.C.L.E.

Michael Avallone

Based on the MGM television series
The Man From U.N.C.L.E.

ACE BOOKS, INC.
1120 Avenue of the Americas
New York, N.Y. 10036.

THE MAN FROM U.N.C.L.E.

Copyright © 1965, by Metro-Goldwyn-Mayer Inc.

DEDICATION:

For my brother Pat—
who never lost his smile.

THE U.N.C.L.E. ORGANIZATION

(United Network Command for Law and Enforcement)

THERE IS A ROW of buildings in New York City, a few blocks from the United Nations Building. At the south end of the row is a three-storied whitestone which appears fairly new in comparison to the brownstone buildings which make up the rest of the street. At the north end is a public garage. The brownstones are occupied by a few lower-income families living above the decrepit shops and businesses which rent the space on the street level. Del Floria's tailor shop occupies the street level space in a brownstone near the middle of the block. The first and second floors of the whitestone are taken up by an exclusive key-club restaurant known as *The Masked Club*.

On the third floor of the whitestone is a sedate suite of offices the entrance to which bears the engraved letters "U.N.C.L.E." In this suite of offices, a rather ordinary group of people handle mail, meet and do business with visitors, and in general seem to be a normal organization engaged in some special charity project or a Fund Foundation operation.

All these buildings are owned by the organization known as U.N.C.L.E.

If it were possible to peel away the outer, decaying brownstone skin of the four old buildings, a surprising edifice would be found. For behind the walls is one large building consisting of a complex modern office setup of three floors: a steel maze of corridors and suites containing brisk, alert young personnel of many races, creeds and backgrounds . . . as well as complex masses of modern machinery and equipment, all of a highly technological nature.

There are no staircases in the building. Four elevators handle vertical traffic.

Below the basement level an underground channel has been cut through from the East River, leading out to sea. On the roof of the building is a large neon-lighted advertising billboard whose supporting pillars contain a high-powered short-wave antenna as well as elaborate receiving and sending gear.

This is the heart, brain and body of the organization named U.N.C.L.E.

The personnel of the organization is peculiarly multinational. And their line of work tends to cross national boundaries with such nonchalance that a daily short-wave message from the remote Himalayas fails to flutter any eyebrows—this even though there is no recorded wireless in this Himalayan area according to the printed international codebooks.

An Organization Chart for U.N.C.L.E. would read as follows:

SECTION I:	Policy and Operations
SECTION II:	Operations and Enforcement
SECTION III:	Enforcement and Communications
SECTION IV:	Communications and Security
SECTION V:	Security and Personnel

Napoleon Solo is the Chief Enforcement Agent for U.N.C.L.E.

THE THOUSAND COFFINS AFFAIR

WHAT HAPPENED TO STEWART FROMES?

A CORPSE is always interesting.

Rich man, poor man, beggar man or king, who a man is and how he died is of far greater interest to mortal man than, say, the price of eggs in Istanbul. The corpse that comes into being for strange and exotic reasons, of course, is of paramount interest to the police and law enforcement agencies of the world. And while all of us are touched in some phantom way because another human being has been singled out by the Grim Reaper, the death of a special agent is naturally a vital matter to the body of men of which the corpse was a member.

Stewart Fromes was just such a man. Just such a corpse.

Fromes died in Oberteisendorf, Germany at approximately five-fifteen (German Central Time). He was 37, in excellent physical condition, a master field chemist for the organization known as U.N.C.L.E. In Korea, he had won a Silver Star for staying seven days on Heartbreak Ridge before a hand grenade put him out of action. In Oberteisendorf, there were no battles and no medals.

There was only the long, unending far-into-the-night research which had brought him to the little town below the Bavarian Alps in the first place.

On the day he was to die, he did three interesting things.

At five o'clock that last afternoon, Stewart Fromes was taking a bath in the wooden tub placed at the rear of the tiny laboratory he had set up in Frau Morganstern's home. He was thoughtfully soaping his lean, angular body when he experienced the odd dizziness which had become particularly chronic this past week.

Fromes waited no longer. He stepped naked from the tub, heedless of the soap and the chill of the drafty house. His bare feet sloshed across the wooden floor to the rear of the laboratory. There, a rickety wooden cage revealed a carrier pigeon nestling quietly. With quick, deliberate movements, Fromes affixed a tiny banded scroll to the pigeon's right claw and set it free. He hardly waited to see it spring for the Eastern sky, its wings fluttering rapidly.

The second interesting thing that Stewart Fromes did was to suddenly fall flat on his face in the center of the room, kicking over a low table on which he had set his clothes. He began to thrash about violently, his arms and legs twitching uncontrollably. Had anyone been present, he would have been amazed and terribly frightened to hear Stewart Fromes, third in the '47 Class of Cornell, begin to babble incoherently. The walls of the laboratory echoed with a string of moaning, gibbering sounds. The dampness of his naked body left small patches of moisture wherever his vibrating body touched.

And then Stewart Fromes did the third interesting thing before he died.

Through the haze of pain and the complete seizure of his limbs and muscles, he reached blindly for the clothing scattered on the floor—his coat, trousers and shirt, which had toppled from the low table.

Stewart Fromes was dying. Slowly. Terribly.

Yet even as he rolled around on the floor like a frenzied mad dog, he began to *dress*.

Alexander Waverly, fingering one of his many unsmoked pipes in the quiet office of the U.N.C.L.E. building in New York, was unhappy. As head of Policy and Operations, he was no alarmist. Yet the transatlantic message from Paris Headquarters had been upsetting. Stewart Fromes had been on to something; that had been most apparent from his reports of the last few hectic weeks. Now, suddenly, he was dead.

Five men, of various nationalities, guided the Policy operations of U.N.C.L.E. Waverly was one of that very select five. Yet a casual observer would be forgiven if he thought this elderly-looking man to be a gentle old college professor who tended toward crabbiness.

Waverly pocketed his cold briar pipe and walked to the wide, high window of his office—the only window in the entire fortress known as U.N.C.L.E. Before him spread a sunny panoramic view of the United Nations Building, poking like a modernistic glass finger from the depths of the East River.

"Napoleon Solo," Waverly said aloud. "Of course."

The Fromes affair was obviously a matter which called for the special talents of the chief enforcement officer of U.N.C.L.E.

Clucking to himself as if chiding a personal error, he hurried back to his desk. A row of five enamel buttons lay at right angles to his fingertips: one orange, one red, one gold, one blue, one yellow. Waverly thumbed the blue one.

There was a *click* as a connection was made somewhere in the office. A smooth, unworried voice abruptly filled the room, seeming to emerge from the four walls: *"Section IV."*

"Cablegram," Waverly said, putting his forefinger to his nose. "Napoleon Solo, Hotel Internationale, Paris."

"Yes, Mr. Waverly."

"Fromes Dead In Oberteisendorf, Germany. Claim Body Immediately. Your Uncle Greatly Upset." Waverly paused. "Remember To Call His Mother. William Daprato Sends His Best."

"Is there more to the message, Sir?"

"No, that's all. Do you want me to repeat any of it?"

"No, Sir."

Waverly thumbed the blue button again. He smiled, thinking about Solo. If past performances were any yardstick, Solo had already found Paris a most charming place to be on assignment. He'd much rather his top agent spend more time on enhancing his mind—at the Louvre, say, or even the Left Bank—but Solo was one of those young men eternally inclined to study the opposite sex.

Waverly snorted to himself, turning to the mystery of Stewart Fromes' sudden, untimely demise.

That was something that demanded his immediate attention.

"Anything wrong, Napoleon? You look so worried. Is the cablegram bad news of some kind?"

"No. But I *would* like you to excuse me for a minute or so. A business matter, pet."

"Napoleon, look at me. Is that from another woman?"

Napoleon Solo studied the long-legged brunette raising herself from a langorous position on the gilded love seat. Denise Fairmount was worth more than one look. Her amber eyes looked beautiful even in anger. Her silver lamé gown shimmered as she rose, emphasizing the almost feline beauty of her body. Solo reflected briefly that the Hotel Internationale's plush, brocaded Suite Four One One was a completely appropriate setting for her. She was like some regal holdover from another century of French beauty—with just enough Americanizing to make her doubly interesting.

He smiled at her. "If the cablegram were from another woman, I'd simply tear it up and put on another long-playing record."

She lifted her chin, eyes sparkling.

"Very well then. Go read your important cablegram in privacy. I'll mix us another *aperitif*. We can get back to where we were—soon enough, *n'est-ce-pas?*"

He winked. "Be back in a jiffy, Beautiful."

She nodded, watching him move toward the bedroom. The yellowish lights of the suite seemed to cast a halation around Napoleon Solo's form. Denise Fairmount sighed softly, and shook her head, bewildered by the unexpected sexual appeal of this man.

He had become far more than she had bargained for. Yesterday, on the Champs d'Elysée, she had picked him up as he sauntered on the sunny thoroughfare. He had been easy to pick out of the crowd of tourists on a spree. The foolishness she had invented about lost directions had not deceived him, she knew. She had not intended that they should. And so they had flirted, dined at Maxim's that evening . . . and that was that. They had spent the night here in Suite Four One One.

She shivered in memory. An interesting man, Solo. An extraordinary charmer. It was a pity that he would have to die.

In the bedroom, Solo moved like a cat. His movements reflected tensile strength and an economy of effort that marked him for the trained athlete he was. His face, oddly boyish and pleasant, could become a cold mask of intellectual resolve when he was not smiling.

He was not smiling now.

Waverly's cablegram, held under a bedlamp, was upsetting:

NAPOLEON SOLO
HOTEL INTERNATIONALE PARIS FRANCE

FROMES DEAD IN OBERTEISENDORF GERMANY CLAIM BODY IMMEDIATELY YOUR UNCLE GREATLY UPSET REMEMBER TO CALL HIS MOTHER WILLIAM DAPRATO SENDS HIS BEST
WAVERLY

Stewart Fromes was dead. Solo scowled and the lines in his face hardened.

William Daprato sends his best.

It was quite unlike Waverly to be so cryptic in a straight, harmless telegram. The death of Fromes was a blow, of course—a very personal one which Solo, who had known and liked the man, felt deeply. But the reference to Bill Daprato was something else again.

"Booby traps for booby traps," Solo said, tasting each word as he said it. That was Bill Daprato's best—the one GI line of advice to all combat rookies. Solo folded the cablegram and put it into his coat pocket. There was something damnedably odd—

Before he could further explore the meaning of Waverly's message, Denise Fairmount screamed shrilly from the living room.

A high, thin scream of mortal terror.

"SOME OF MY BEST FRIENDS ARE SPIES"

SOLO REACHED the door of the bedroom in something less than one second, and he paused there, his eyes taking in the scene in quick, darting glances.

At first, the tableau seemed just as it had been when he'd left. Denise was still half-reclining on the love seat —but now every line and angle of her body was taut, frozen, as if she dared not make the slightest movement. Her beautiful face was a pinched mask of horror. The amber eyes seemed fixed on a point before her, between the love seat and the carved oak coffee table. Her hands were clutching the golden bolsters of the chair.

Yet there was nothing in the room.

19

Solo eased toward her, his hand streaking reflexively for his shoulder holster. He restrained a low curse, realizing that the romantic tenor of the evening had made him injudicious enough to leave his gun somewhere other than on his person. Moving closer he held his breath, his eyes on the woman.

It was then that the *noise* came to him. Suddenly, unbearably, there was a tingling sensation in his eardrums—a light, almost feathery sound of some kind like the low hum of a generator. He stopped short. Denise Fairmount moaned.

"My ears—oh, my God . . ." It was a cry of agony.

Solo shook his head, trying to clear it. The tingling feeling had begun to expand so that his brain seemed alive with the concerted buzz of a horde of bees. He felt his body tremble violently.

Denise had begun to writhe in torment. And still the low, humming, throbbing sound continued—rising in volume so that it filled the entire room.

The lights danced before Solo's straining vision. The details of the room—the furniture and the drapes and the paintings—tilted with alarming abruptness. The floor seemed to move beneath his feet. The maroon carpet twisted in Daliesque convolutions. The sound expanded, moving to the walls as though it were something solid that needed a vessel to contain it.

Solo staggered, fighting the waves of dizziness that rolled over him. It was difficult to breathe now. His hearing had magnified so that the slightest tremor of the *sound* made him want to scream, to run, to hide. Panic tried to hold him, arrest his mind.

The hum of sound grew louder.

Solo moved with fierce momentum. He hurled him-

self toward the wall near the door. Still the noise in his
head rose with tremendous shrieking violence. He fell
down, literally hammered to his knees by the force of
the sound. Yet he crawled to the base of the wall, and
his dazed eyes found the square metal frame that housed
the wall plug. Thank God, it was not in use.

Working in a screaming, smothering blanket of pain,
his hands shaking almost uncontrollably, he managed to
find his key chain. With a last thrust of concentrated
will, he rammed the first one he found into the exposed
wall circuit.

There was a blinding, flashing crackle of blue flame,
and he was flung back from the wall by the short-cir-
cuiting electrical currents. The room plunged into darkness. Sudden, inky midnight.

And the sound stopped.

Solo lay on the floor, his face ground into the carpet-
ing. Waves of relief rolled over him. His body stilled as
the humming, throbbing noise receded like the distant,
fading sound of a jet engine. The abrupt silence was
nearly as stupifying as the humming itself had been.

For awhile, there was only the racking, terrible sobbing of the girl on the love seat.

The blinding pain that had filled his head faded in the
wake of the sound, leaving only a sense of utter weariness and near demoralization. Solo remained on the
floor, breathing in great gulps of air. He could feel his
heart beating furiously. And then, that slowed down too.
The only thing that remained of the awesome sound
was an amazing sensation of the noises of the sea batter-
ing a shoreline.

Later—he could not tell exactly how much later—he
got to his feet. He reached into his pocket, drew out a

pencil flash, and thumbed it on. It showed him Denise Fairmount lying exhausted on the lounge. He shook himself, moving unsteadily to the escritoire on the opposite wall. His gun was in the top drawer.

It was more Luger than anything else, bearing a slight resemblance to the P-38 of World War Two origin. Solo's automatic was unique, however. There was an engraved letter "S" stamped on the heavy butt. He couldn't remember when he had ever felt more relieved to have it in his hand. The persistent, piercing sound had rocked him as few things ever had.

He returned to the girl, after he had found one of the ornamental candelabra on the marble mantlepiece in the center of the room. Candlelight would have to do now that the electrical power in the suite was out.

In any other circumstances, Denise Fairmount would have looked enticing by candlelight. The spray of burning radiance washed over her curves, making her body gleam invitingly. Solo stared down at her.

"Wake up," he said coldly, prodding her with his free hand. "The Steinmetz Exhibit is over."

She groaned, her eyelashes fluttering.

"Rise and shine, Denise. We have to talk a bit."

She opened her eyes. She swallowed hard, looking at him.

"Oh God—my ears ached so—"

"My ears too. Where did you put it, pet?"

"Put what?" She blinked up at him.

His smile was icy. "The little gadget known more properly as a transistor. Probably no larger than a woman's earring. You going to tell me or shall I start pulling your arms and legs off right now?"

"Napoleon, I—" She started to rise, almost angrily, and

he pushed her back. "I don't know what you mean," she protested. "I was in this room, too."

"Yes," he agreed amiably. "That's the way your play-mates operate. Which means you can't be very impor-tant, or else you goofed personally on this whole setup. Okay. I'll play A B C with you. A—my electronic friends tell me that electricity can be converted into sound with a fancy little thing called the *maser*, an incredibly sensitive amplifier. B.—if that sound had continued, there's no telling what it would have done to your nerv-ous system and mine, so I stopped the noise by cutting the electrical current in this room. C.—you have the transistor or you know where it is. Simple ABC, isn't it?"

She shuddered, trying to smile.

"What do you think I am, Napoleon?"

"A spy, of course. But don't let that bother you. Some of my best friends are spies."

She nodded, hardly hearing him. "All right. But you'll have to believe me when I tell you I have no idea about any transistor." Her smile was wan. "As you say, they think little of me. Or else they think so highly of you that they'd sacrifice me too."

His eyes narrowed. A decoy again. A lovely lure. Nothing new for him, surely. He knew that Denise Fair-mount had maneuvered him into a defenseless position for the kill. He had known that was her purpose yester-day when he had allowed her to pick him up. But he had his own plans—like pumping her for information.

"Who do you work for, Denise? Thrush?"

She shook her head. "I will tell you nothing."

"All right. We'll skip the third degree. There are other things to occupy my time. Stand up."

There was no use browbeating her, he had decided.

She was more than just a lovely woman—spying was no business for wilting geraniums. Before he could manage to make her talk, her "friends" would undoubtedly be moving in on him.

She raised herself, staring into his face. The deep cleft of her breasts rose as she breathed deeply. She kept her arms rigid at her sides.

"Well, what is the next move, Mr. Solo?"

He smiled—warmly, but yet faintly mocking. "I thought we might call Room Service for some wine to go with our candlelight."

Her eyes flashed. "Don't insult me by not being serious."

"The serious die young," he said softly.

She frowned, biting her lip. "You must kill me, yes. But if you would delay it for awhile there is much I could do for you. In a personal way, of course."

"I like you too, Denise. So much so that I'm going to make it easy for you."

She misunderstood him, and let herself insinuate her body a bit closer. She moistened her lips, tilting her chin.

He hit her.

The blow was short, swift, economical—a precisely-timed and aimed uppercut which collapsed Denise Fairmount neatly on the love seat. She fell without even a murmur of surprise. He arranged her carefully on the lounge, lowering her lamé gown chastely below her knees.

There was no more time for delays. He had risked enough already. Nor could he encumber himself with lovely lady agents, no matter who they might be. Waverly's cablegram was burning a hole in his pocket. If the

Fairmount woman had anything to do with that assignment, he would find out soon enough. Meanwhile, he was in a vicinity he should quit as soon as possible. Thrush, if Thrush it was, had a way of reinforcing its death traps in a hurry.

There had been no hue and cry from the rest of the hotel.

Perhaps a blessing. Perhaps not.

Soundlessly and swiftly, Solo packed his sky-blue traveling suitcase and checked the windows. The suite opened on a sheer ledge above the lighted boulevard. Time enough to call in and have somebody pick up the Fairmount woman. His first concern had to be getting out of the hotel with all of his skin—and, preferably, everything still inside it.

He glanced at Denise on the lounge. In the glow of the candles on the oaken coffee table, she was beautifully innocent and serene. Solo's eyes hardened. He moved toward the door, putting her out of his mind. She was a regret better left unfelt.

He turned the door handle and—nothing happened. He tried it again, but it still wouldn't open. Alarm bells began ringing in the back of his mind. Slowly, he set the suitcase down and studied the door. His eyes traveled around the seaming where the wood met the wall. A feeling that something wasn't quite right or proper filled him. He bent closer to examine the tiny vertical and horizontal cracks which allowed the door barrier to fit perfectly into the design of the room.

The door was sealed! No air was coming in from the passageway. It was as if the frame of the portal had been sealed with putty or wax. But it had to be more than that—

He took an identification card from his wallet—it was one of several, this one certifying that he was one Arthur Connell, an authorized buyer for an expensive-sounding New York jeweler—and tried to thrust it between door and wall. The card did not pass through the slit. Something was preventing it from finding an entry; it was as if a sheet of metal had passed over the outer doorway—

A sliding, scratching sound, as of something traveling with mechanical ease into a slotted groove, made his head swing toward the big windows.

Incredibly, he saw the bright lights of Paris wink out as a partition of metal moved quickly across his line of vision and snapped shut with a click of sound like the closing of a cigarette case.

A moment later, another sheet of metal closed off the window on the other side of the room, gliding smoothly into its metallic bed. Whirling, he saw the open doorway into the bedroom closed off and sealed by a final metal slab.

Suddenly the room was like a soundless vacuum. Denise lay unconscious on the lounge, and Solo stood frozen for the moment. The short hairs at the nape of his neck tingled. There was no mistaking this new threat now.

Unless he was badly mistaken, the room had suddenly become an air-tight vault. There could be no other reason for the complete sealing of both the doors and windows. Locks would have been enough to trap him inside —but Thrush didn't want him simply as a prisoner. They wanted him dead.

He was trapped in a sealed room in which the supply of usable, life-giving oxygen would diminish into nothingness.

Then the silence of the room was broken by a subtle soughing sound—the sound of air whispering through an opening somewhere. Solo's hand jerked around, following the sound, and then he saw it. A wave of relief flooded over him. Of course—the air-conditioning system! Even though they had sealed the immediately obvious sources of air, the members of Thrush had forgotten that all the rooms in the hotel had completely up-to-date air-conditioning.

He smiled as he stepped toward the vent. Such a simple mistake . . . but of course the simple things were the most easy to forget.

He put his hand up to the vent—and the smile disappeared from his face.

Thrush hadn't forgotten the air-conditioning at all. Instead, they were using it themselves. For there was no air coming into the room—instead, it was steadily being sucked *out*.

THE DEATH ROOM

For one wild second, a sense of doom fought to dominate him. Thrush had bottled him up like a mouse in a Mason jar and no amount of banging away at the lid was going to help. There was no time to lose now. No reason to stop and wonder just how long a man can live without oxygen or how long it would take for the vent to pump out every bit of good air left in the room. Time enough for post-mortems later.

Getting out of the room was the first order of the day.

He considered the possible means of escape. There was, of course, the telephone—but when he picked it up he found the line was dead. He wasn't surprised. It would also be useless to use his machine pistol. No amount of bullets could blow that door—nor any of the windows. He silently cursed the lack of any explosive equipment in his suitcase. This was one time he had none of the jelly compounds that could blow a bank vault wall to smithereens. He hadn't expected to have to enter any bank vaults this week—much less that he'd find himself trapped *inside* one.

There was only one chance.

The very one that Thrush itself had given him.

Solo hurried to Denise Fairmount where she lay on the lounge. Her head lolled as he pulled her to a standing position. He brought his open hand sharply against her face, slapping her quickly on both sides of her nose. She moaned and he dragged her to the coffee table, scooping up the bottle of wine. He held it to her lips, forcing the contents into her mouth. The wine sloshed over her face, ran down the front of her gown. Solo paid little heed. He wanted this woman awake, sitting up and taking notice—

Already, he could sense the change in the atmosphere of the room. There was a sudden giddiness in his head —a light, airy feeling as though he had had too much of the same wine he was pouring over the woman. She stirred, and coughed as the wine went down her throat.

"Come on, Denise," he snapped. "Wake up, wake up!"

"What—what—" She sputtered, her eyes opening wide, blanching when she saw him, trying to pull away.

He gripped her wrists tightly, keeping his voice steady.

"Listen. I'm not going to hurt you. Are you awake? Nod your head so that I know you understand me. Nod, I said!" He jerked her savagely to him. Her eyes popped but she nodded, her tongue licking at the droplets of wine on her mouth.

"Your playmates have walled us up in this room. With steel doors and windows and everything. You understand? There'll be no air to speak of in here in a very little while—they're also sucking the air out through the air-conditioning vent. I know of a way we can get out— but you've got to help. Listen to me, Denise. We will slowly suffocate to death without oxygen. You won't look pretty to the undertaker with your tongue sticking out. Now tell me—where is that transistor for the master device? I must know—or we're both going to die."

"You're trying to trick me—" she gasped. "You hit me —"

"Nod, I said. Don't waste air with talking. Breathe. Can't you tell? Come on, Denise. Where is it?"

She read his eyes and she read the warning there. She nodded and her own gaze swung back to the coffee table. Not on top of it. *Under it.* The candles had already begun to gutter warningly. Solo released the woman and darted to the table. He explored its bottom quickly until his hands found a square metal box, no bigger than the motor of a tiny music box. Denise Fairmount had fallen to the lounge, breathing in short, shallow gasps. Solo ignored her and ripped open his traveling bag. He knew what he had to do. A risk he had to

29

take. There was no estimating the effect of the maser device when let loose—*but he knew what it could do.*

He scooped his neatly piled clothes to one side and uncovered the short-wave radio set hidden there. He had short-circuited the suite's electrical outlet, but the radio set had its own powerful batteries. He hoped they would be strong enough for what he had in mind.

He placed the maser device at the very center of the front door, between the sealed slit and the bottom of the barrier. Then he adjusted the short-wave set, turned it on and manipulated the frequency button. He pushed it to its fullest power. Then he yelled on last warning at Denise Fairmount: "Put your fingers in your ears! This is going to be rough!"

Almost immediately, the wildly throbbing humming sound of generated sound rose in the stuffy room. Solo held his ears tightly, his eyes never leaving the door. He remained by his suitcase. If it didn't work, at least he could turn the sound off before that killed them first. A small difference in terrible ways to die—

But the maser device was trained directly on the door; the sound which buffeted him and Denise was only that which bounced off and spread around the room.

He watched the door. He felt the room tremble. He could see the objects of furniture in the room start that weird vibrating dance again as the sound waves reached them. He bit his lip, beads of perspiration popping on his brow. It was a million to one shot—could the heightening of electrical current into sound force open a steel barrier?

Denise Fairmount was again writhing in pain on the lounge, her eyes two beacons of shining terror. But she did not cry out or protest—she knew what was at stake.

Solo waited—

The furnishings danced. And then a slight tremor shook the door. The hinges seemed to want to move out of their iron hasps. Even with his hands pressed to his ears, the room-filling sound penetrated almost maddeningly.

Solo's nostrils and throat ached with the pain of trying to breathe the thin air remaining now in the sealed room. He felt as though he were being strangled. Yet he could not take his eyes off that door—

It was like a magic act.

Suddenly the door was shaking and the panels warping before his very eyes. And then there was a mammoth thunderclap of sound, and the barrier had surged outward, crumpling like so much cheap tin and discarded metal. The door flew back, ripping off its hinges, shattering into splinters against the sheet of metal which was disintegrating before it.

Groping almost blindly, Solo found the frequency button and turned the short-wave radio set off. The influx of air from the corridor was a buffeting wind which threw over the candles from the table and flattened the drapes against the far wall. He didn't waste any time looking for the maser device in the wreckage of the doorway. Chances were pretty good that it had shattered into bits once its maximum peak of effect had been reached. As for the woman—

She was gone.

In the decreasing flurry of noises from the blasted threshold of the room, he could hear her high heels running down the corridor. For a fleeting second he considered giving chase, but then he shook the notion off. There was only one thing for him to do now—get out of this damn hotel alive before Thrush came back to try again.

Shaking his head to clear it, breathing in long gasps of fresh air, he retrieved his traveling bag and stepped quickly from the room. The aftermath of the explosion was reaching that point when rudely-disturbed guests would be ringing the desk to see what the hell was going on.

Solo took the back stairway out.

Twenty minutes later, he had compartmentalized the anger in his mind and found a late-cruising taxicab on short notice. The tinseled lights of the Eiffel Tower burst like a Fourth of July sparkler on the horizon. Solo had brushed his hair back, straightened his tie and assumed the demeanor of pure tourist. The French cabbie was a gray little man with a wise face and a gold tooth.

"Monsieur?"

"Le Bourget. *Tout de suite.*"

The cabbie looked dismayed.

"You are meeting a plane? None at this time."

"I am taking a plane, my friend."

The cabbie smiled triumphantly. *"Mais non,* Monsieur. There will be none at this hour."

Solo frowned. He knew the Paris airport as well as he knew La Guardia. Flights nearly every hour. He plucked a crisp five hundred franc note from his billfold.

"Look, garçon. Just drive, will you?"

The driver turned around to show appreciation of the bill; yet there was a touch of sadness in his eyes.

"Possibly Monsieur has not heard."

"Let me hear it."

"Le Bourget had the big explosion a few hours ago.

Five runways were destroyed. Such a fire! All flights have been canceled. You understand?"

"Yeah. Pay now. Fly later."

"*Comment?*"

Solo nodded, keeping his face blank. "Yes, I understand, friend. But don't you recognize a newspaperman when you see one? I'll have you know I'm the Paris correspondent to *The New York Times.*"

"*The New York Times?*" The cabbie's eyes rolled in appreciation of such lofty environs. "Forgive me, Monsieur. But of course. *Immediatement!*"

The cab leaped into gear, found the main artery of traffic and zoomed toward Le Bourget. Napoleon Solo drummed his fingers reflectively on the sky-blue Tourister sitting across his lap.

Now here was calamity piled atop coincidence.

A cablegram from Mr. Waverly and a concerted effort on his life.

Now, he needed an airplane and Le Bourget was incapacitated. Of course, there might be other, smaller fields in Paris, yet that was unlikely.

What had happened to Stewart Fromes out there in Oberteisendorf?

The telegram in his coat pocket was beginning to burn a hole there. Hot stuff, maybe. Real hot stuff. Hotter than even Mr. Waverly had let on, despite the William Daprato warning.

Beyond the cab's window, the Paris night twinkled with warm, friendly stars.

At U.N.C.L.E. Headquarters, Alexander Waverly had a visitor. A distinguished visitor whose presence would normally have occasioned the unified popping of assorted flashbulbs and trained questions by batteries of metropolitan reporters. No one in the building was even aware of the identity of this particular individual. He had entered U.N.C.L.E. in Waverly's private elevator from the entranceway which no other man in the organization knew. Only Waverly could ever reveal the fifth unknown ingress of U.N.C.L.E.

Had Napoleon Solo been on hand, he would have been surprised at the difference in Waverly's attitude. It was marked by a definite concern, a worried crease of the gray brows above the strong nose.

Waverly's visitor was at the window, seemingly lost in contemplation of the United Nations Building shining in the night. The long, erratic conga of lights lighting up the Queens skyline hung like fireflies in the far off darkness.

The eternal pipe, in this instance a meerschaum, worked back and forth in Waverly's fingers, revealing his agitation.

The man at the window, tall and statuesque, said without turning, "Well, Waverly. Is there one chance in ten million?"

Waverly did not turn around either.

"There's always *that* chance, of course," he said, regretfully.

"If even that chance is there, then we indeed have something to worry about."

"I would say so, Sir. Fromes was not explicit, of course. He couldn't afford to be, under the circumstances. Security has its drawbacks. But—"

"Go on, Waverly. Say it. Say it all. This is no damn

time for the niceties of protocol and diplomatic bush-wah."

Waverly swiveled in his armchair and pointed the meerschaum for emphasis. "Fromes gave me enough data to suspect the worst. If Thrush has come up with such a weapon—and there *is* evidence to support their participation in this business—then we have something far worse to worry about than missiles and nuclear war."

The man at the window faced Waverly. His face was hidden in the half-light of the room.

"You mean that obscure African village—Utangaville, was it? And Spayerville in the highlands of Scotland."

"Yes, yes," Waverly said, almost impatiently. "If they can destroy towns like that with a mere thimbleful of the stuff, there's no estimating the consequences. Test towns, pure and simple. Places that would not attract the notice of the world. What else? Typical Thrush tactics, Sir. We have to be prepared for the worst."

The visitor shook himself. His voice rose, almost sadly.

"I have a large illumined globe of the world in my office. A gift of the people who pay the taxes. Now, there is a nation named Thrush in the world. You know it and I know it. Yet if we were to examine that globe as carefully as possible, we wouldn't find the name engraved anywhere. And time and again, I've passed my fingers over that globe, on country after country, never really knowing which one has become a territory under the domination of Thrush. *Satraps,* my political advisors call them—satraps for the supra-nation we call Thrush. And they intend to dominate the earth. By degrees, they can turn a country into a satrap—or do the same with a school or a hospital. Or an industrial plant. Who knows? And all we can do is sit, wonder and play international chess while they work underground. Waverly, Waverly —what can we do this time?"

Waverly rubbed his pipe.

"The recovery of Fromes' body is all we can do at this point, Sir."

"No ideas at all what killed him?"

"The laboratory will have to answer that. The acquisition of his body is our first and only step."

The distinguished visitor shook his head.

"I wish I could share your enthusiasm, Waverly. Were the corpse that important, they wouldn't have been so cooperative about returning it, don't you think?"

"Hard to say. Blocking our efforts to do so might have proved more dangerous."

"I'm sure you know what you're talking about. I tend to high pessimism these days." The man straightened. "Who is claiming Fromes' body?"

Waverly's gloomy face brightened a trifle.

"Solo. My best man."

"Odd name. Well, Waverly, I'd best be going. You'll keep me up-to-the-minute on this, I trust? I have my own VIP's to keep alerted."

"Of course, Sir."

Both men shook hands warmly.

"Waverly."

"Yes?"

"It is a comfort that U.N.C.L.E. exists. A far greater comfort than I can ever publicly laud or acknowledge. Do you understand?"

"I think so, Sir. Thank you."

Waverly was still fingering his pipe in happy memory of what the man had said long after the secret elevator had whisked its important passenger down to the underground garage where the Secret Service agents waited. Fromes' body was the key to the whole Thrush matter. And Napoleon Solo was the man to turn that key.

SHADOWS OVER OBERTEISENDORF

LE BOURGET WAS a red glare against the inky backdrop of the Paris sky. Blinding, powerful arc lights traversed the airdrome. A long line of fire trucks and police cars filled the perimeter of the terminal. It was quite like the night Lindbergh had landed on his historic one-man solo flight from New York to Paris. Hordes of onlookers thronged the outskirts of the field, their jostling and shouting drowning out all sanity and order.

Napoleon Solo dismissed the cab driver and alighted. The front doors of the terminal were yet a good quarter of a mile away. Though it was fairly obvious that normal civilian entry was now impossible, Solo walked slowly in that direction. He only paused when he found one of those glass-walled telephone booths. Amidst the hubbub and uproar, he was but another meaningless figure added to the bedlam. The night was alive with sound and fury. It was impossible to estimate exactly what had occurred. An explosion, the cab driver had said. Accident or sabotage?

Solo dodged a trio of hurrying, overalled, grease-stained men, and stepped into the booth. He dropped a coin into the slot and waited. When an operator answered, he asked for a number in the Overseas Press Club. Soon he was connected with a man named Partridge.

"Partridge here," a British accented voice said.

"What is good for hives, Mr. Partridge?"

"Bees."

"What flies forever and rests never?"

"The wind."

"When is a door not a door?"

"When it is ajar."

Solo breathed easy. The simple code, though no great shakes, was unfailing.

"Billy, Le Bourget is in flames."

Partridge's chuckle was grimly unhumorous.

"Indubitably, old sport. Somebody set off a few big ones on the runways at seven this evening. Anything to do with you?"

"It's a possibility. I am supposed to fly out of here."

"What's your destination?"

"Hitler's backyard. Any ideas? Time is, as they say, of the essence."

He could almost hear Partridge thinking before the answer came. The ex-Major Partridge of British Army Intelligence was U.N.C.L.E.'s liaison man in Paris, a safety guarantee factor for just such exigencies as this one.

"Got a car?"

"I'm walking so far."

"I see. How far into the backyard are you going?"

"The Redoubt. I'm picking up Fromes."

"Listen carefully." Partridge spoke quickly now.

"There's an air strip at the northeastern tip of Rouen. Nothing much. But a Frenchman named Landry will rent you a plane for a price. Good man. No political convictions save money. Try him."

"That's fine. How do you suggest I get to Rouen?"

"Hmmm." There was another pause. "Where are you now?"

Solo peered through the glass walls of his booth. There was a painted sign and a number staring down at him from the stucco side of a shed of some kind.

"Le Bourget. Tool shed seven-oh-three-three-nine. About five hundred yards from the eastern approach to the main terminal."

"Stay put. A jeep will be there directly. You may leave it with Monsieur Landry."

"Partridge, I love you."

"Don't mention it. And I *am* sorry about Fromes. He was a decent chap."

Napoleon Solo hung up soberly, staring for a moment at the silent phone box. A *decent chap*. A glorious testimonial to a man who had given his life for his country. Fromes would understand though. There were no medals, no financial bonuses, no awards to win with U.N.C.L.E. Only the memory of men like Partridge.

Outside the booth, the thick aroma of smoke mixed with gasoline and oil assaulted his nostrils. He winced, turning up his collar. The night air was biting, despite the proximity of the smoldering blaze igniting the area as far as the eye could see.

Sighing philosophically, he fished out a pack of French cigarettes and lit one from his jet-flame lighter. He reversed his Tourister on the shorter end and sat down to wait.

All about him, Le Bourget was a madhouse.

To American GI's of World War Two, Rouen had been easily, almost charitably, dubbed The Road to Ruin. For it was here that the long march into Germany to end the combat in the European Theater of Operations usually began. Once troopships landed at devastated Le Havre, Rouen was the first step on the leg of the journey for all ETO Task Forces. Solo had served in Korea, being but a stripling in the days of Pearl Harbor, but many a retread on Heartbreak Ridge had regaled him with yarns about Rouen. Armored Division men had long memories, and their GI French was interwoven with the history of the little border city just outside the harbor. Patton had filled his gas tanks there; every Army of the U.S. that swept through fortress Europe had known Rouen for at least a day.

Now, as he wheeled the jeep swiftly over the unpaved roads, with forests of trees engulfing him on either side, Solo thought about Waverly's cryptic note. Memories of Rouen had recalled William Daprato, the combat M.P. to whom Waverly had referred in his cable. Daprato had been in Rouen. His outfit had landed there after a stint in North Africa. It was here that his poignant warning had been given birth.

A squad of his men had entered a bistro on a mop-up campaign following the German evacuation of the town. When one unwary M.P. had picked up a bottle of Pommard wine and foolishly tugged up the cork, there had been little left of the soldier save a bloody mass of flesh. *"Booby traps for booby troops,"* Corporal Daprato had cursed bitterly. The remark had become legendary—filtering down through the ranks, the divisions, the platoons and squads until one night it had reached the ears of First Lieutenant Napoleon Solo, First Cavalry Regiment. He had burned the remark into his consciousness of war. When the time came for his fitness report as a member of U.N.C.L.E., it had been included as code information on his file. Hence the simple use of the name *William Daprato* meant a volume of words— a code no enemy could ever break because it only meant something to Napoleon Solo.

But what did its usage mean in the assignment of recovering Stewart Fromes' corpse? Did Waverly actually mean to suggest that he thought Fromes' body was mined in some way? That was ridiculous—or was it? Still, it was something to think about, wasn't it?

Solo thought a great deal about it as he spurred the jeep along, the needle far beyond the 60 mile mark. The mechanized bug shot over the road, whipping like the mechanical rabbit at a quinella. The slipstream flung Solo's tie like a pennant in the breeze.

The stars had vanished behind a sudden all-enveloping darkness. It was hazardous going. Solo peered carefully through the windshield, his eyes alert to abrupt dips and bends in the roadway.

Partridge's jeep had been delivered by a silent U.S. Army sergeant who had done little more than turn over the ignition keys and make an idle comment about the Le Bourget fire. Partridge had his own methods, obviously. Solo had quit the vicinity of the airfield as soon as was possible. He hadn't quite forgotten the nasty set-to in Denise Fairmount's company. Something was up all right, and it all seemed to point to Stewart Fromes— and/or Thrush.

Bright lights winked up ahead. Rouen.

Solo slowed for a high grade, put the jeep in low gear and rose sharply. The lights were to his left. He consulted his watch. Close to ten-thirty. He found a map in the glove compartment of the jeep and scanned it thoroughly. The compass needles set artfully in the watch face indicated northeast. Grimly, he swung the jeep where the road suddenly forked to the right. Landry's airstrip shouldn't be too far away, by his reckoning.

It wasn't.

Past a cluster of houselights and streets of poor illumination, he spotted a dirt road leading to the northeastern end of Rouen, then a bevy of scattered farms. A cow mooed in the night. Solo concentrated. It would be easy to lose sight of his destination in the deepening gloom.

Then he saw what he was looking for: ten kerosene markers glowing in the night. There was a wide expanse of earth lighter-colored than the rest of the brown French ground, then a long, low hangar of sorts. Dimly against the horizon he spotted the trim outlines of the airplane.

Landry was waiting for him.

"You fly, my friend?"

"Yes. I will pay you well."

"Good—on both counts. I am sure you will like the plane we have for you."

The man was a parody of France—fat, bereted, pot-bellied and dirty as a swine. A burned-down cigarette barely peeked from beneath a clump of walrus mustache. Solo's nostrils curled. The man wasn't worth trusting. Yet, Partridge had vouched for him.

"I would like to leave immediately."

"As you will, my friend. The plane is already being warmed up."

Solo reached into his pocket for his billfold. His eyes searched Landry's unkempt face. Landry shrugged his mountainous shoulders.

"I prefer American money if you have it. One thousand dollars will do nicely."

It was Solo's turn to shrug. "Will ten traveler's checks at one hundred each do?"

"Quite nicely, yes."

From outside, came the muted roar of the aircraft. Swiftly, Solo signed ten checks, tore them neatly from the blue folder and handed them to Landry. The Frenchman grunted and tucked them in the waistband of his dirty trousers. Ludicrously, he wore a fashionable cummerbund about his expansive middle.

"How long will the flight take?" Time was the main concern now.

"Where do you journey?"

"Oberteisendorf or any place near enough to make it worthwhile."

Landry considered that. "Three, maybe four hours. As I say, the plane is a good one."

"I'm sure of it. *Au revoir*, my friend."

To Solo's great surprise, he found the plane to be a modern, streamlined Beechcraft Debonair: a real custom-built American job, the plaything of millionaires and Riviera scions. His respect for Landry mounted. He waved back a farewell to the shed where Landry stood at the window.

Solo reached the ship, the fine swath of propellor shining like a million stars in the gloom. He spotted a figure, helmeted and goggled, sitting in the cabin, jerking a gloved thumb at him. Solo pulled the airdoor back and placed his Tourister in the roomy space beyond the two front seats of the cabin job. As he squeezed in, the helmeted figure slid over to the far seat. Solo frowned. Before he could mutter a surprised protest, the short, snout-nosed barrel of an automatic pistol jammed against his midsection.

"Climb in and close the door and don't make any other moves," a bright voice snapped.

Solo's eyes went cold but he did as he was told. The closeness of the cabin made the gun held against his rib cage seem like the bore of a cannon.

"Is this part of Monsieur Landry's plane service?" he asked drily.

"It's my idea," the voice answered. In the gloom of the cabin, he could not make out the face of his captor. "Now prove to me that you are Napoleon Solo. You look like him and you talk like him, but that's not enough. Can you show me some proof?"

Solo sighed and stared straight ahead, eyes probing the night.

"May I reach for my identity card?"

"Go ahead. But no tricks."

Very carefully, he took from his inner pocket a small stack of business cards and plastic-coated licenses, and handed them over.

"Here," he said. "Leaf through those, find the one you want, and perhaps you will win a large, shiny automobile someday."

"You fool!" But his captor said nothing else and took the cards. Solo folded his arms, listening to the smooth tune-up of the Debonair's engine. For a brief second, he watched as the helmeted figure took his U.N.C.L.E.

identity card and applied a small applicator of some kind to its surface. A drop of some form of liquid washed over the face of the card. Nothing happened. There was a satisfied grunt from the occupant of the other seat in the cabin.

"Very good. On all counts. You may take us up now, Mr. Solo. It's time we got out of here."

Solo shrugged and busied himself with the controls. He too wanted to get into the air. He swung the Debonair about, pointing its nose to the East, and began to taxi along the hard, lumpy earth. He checked his instrument panel and hummed to himself. The slender figure at his side had pocketed the snout-nosed automatic quite suddenly.

He drew back gently on the stick, his mind occupied with the takeoff. The nose of the plane knifed forward, seeming to head straight for the high wall of trees before them. Gradually, almost unnoticeably, the wheels left the ground and the Debonair lifted like a graceful bird. The propellor clawed. The instrument gauges danced, the multiple needles busy with recording the flight into darkness.

The dark earth fell away; the trees vanished. Monsieur Landry's fortuitous landing strip faded back into the past.

Solo rubbed at his right eye, yawning, feeling the strain of the night's events. He looked idly at the figure who was now sitting quietly at his side.

"Well, unknown friend and fellow traveler. Are you going to tell me all about it or do we ride in perfect silence the rest of the way?"

His companion's nose, in profile, was as straight as a ruler, the mouth almost lush. A confirming bell went off in Solo's head. He laughed lightly, waiting for the answer to his question.

"You are not a man, I take it. Neither are you somebody who is crazy about airplanes and would do just about anything for a joyride."

The snapping voice laughed back.

"You win, hero. I came here specifically to go with you on your trip. My destination is your destination."

"I see. Will you unmask now or are you going to hide behind the helmet and goggles forever?"

The girl laughed—a warm, vitamin-packed laugh which had all the vigor and go-to-hellishness of a Marine drill sergeant. He looked on admiringly as the helmet and goggles were swept to one side by a long, taperingly-slim hand. Coppery, shoulder-length hair spilled in a golden cascade. A bright, brown-eyed face smiled at him through a chocolate film of grease over the lower half, framing white, impeccable teeth.

"Allow me to introduce myself. This is your co-pilot, Geraldine Terry. On unchartered flight to Oberteisendorf, Germany. I tested your ID card with a special acid and since it didn't corrode, it's the real thing. I didn't kill the man who was supposed to warm up your plane—just cooled him with a little Judo and helped myself to his clothes so that I could get onto the field. Any more questions to relieve your mind?"

He stared at her. It was inconceivable, but there she was. Bright, sunny, a real American Beauty, yet she had maneuvered as sweet a switch as he had ever encountered.

"Geraldine Terry," he mused. "Girl spy?"

"Government girl if you please," she snapped back,

her eyes on the air lanes ahead as if she still didn't trust him. "You can call me Jerry Terry."

The Debonair plunged on smoothly through the night skies over France.

NAPOLEON NO LONGER SOLO

"MORE RAPID than eagles his coursers they came," Solo said quietly. He was smiling slightly, but still on his guard. This could easily be more Denise Fairmount hanky-panky and he hadn't quite reconciled himself to that one yet.

"I beg your pardon, Mr. Solo?" Jerry Terry asked sweetly.

"I was just thinking about the night before Christmas when all sorts of surprises fill my stocking. May I ask why you were so determined to join me on this trip?"

Jerry Terry's smile vanished. It made a startling transformation in her face. The fresh beauty seemed to give way to a Joan of Arc severity.

"That makes sense, Mr. Solo. I am willing to talk. We have a similar interest in this enterprise."

"Go on. I am listening, Miss Terry."

"May I have a cigarette?"

He placed a cigarette between her lips and held his

ligther for her, admiring her features as he did. He decided that the assignment was becoming more interesting all the time.

"All right," he said. "You have your cigarette, we have been informally introduced and you know where I'm going. The question is—who are you and why are you going with me?"

"Solo," she said softly. "I'm not always funny and bright. I'm as responsible as I can be. Stewart Fromes means as much to my organization as it does to yours. Fortunately, both of us are playing on the same side."

"And what is my organization?"

"You're the man from U.N.C.L.E."

"And what is *your* organizatiion?"

"I'm the girl from U.S. Army Intelligence."

Solo frowned. "You'll forgive me, I'm sure, if I find that hard to believe. I never heard of lady intelligence officers."

"They made an exception in my case."

"Why? Are you the G-2's daughter?"

She laughed. "No. But I am young, I am attractive, and I possess the one thing that makes me unique for my job."

"Go ahead," he said. "Hit me. It must be something."

"A photographic memory. A foolproof one, I might add. It has been tested and not been found wanting."

Solo pondered. Yes, that would make her a vital asset to any organization. If she could once look at something —even a maze of blueprint and detail—and record it in her mind as though it were an actual photograph . . . yes, such an agent would be worth her weight in Fort Knox gold.

"All right, Jerry Terry. I'll buy your fish for now. At

least, until we land. But please tell me where this concerns you directly."

She sighed. "Play it cautious. I'll respect you more for it. Very well. We're three thousand feet above the ground and this plane is not bugged or wired for sound. I checked it out while I sat and waited for you. We know about Fromes. We knew he was in Oberteisendorf as a field chemist for U.N.C.L.E. Your people had to let us know about it at the command decision level. It's that big, I understand. We got the report about Fromes' sudden death almost as soon as it happened. The news went through the American Consul to our private line, as it did to yours. Army Intelligence sent me out right away. There may be something vital to memorize in Fromes' laboratory—if they haven't cleaned it out yet."

Solo nodded. "And who do your people think 'they' are?"

Jerry Terry clamped her teeth. "The communists, of course. Who else is so interested in world conquest?"

Solo decided to change the subject.

"What was Fromes working on?"

She shivered. "I don't really know. But, God, it must be big to send all the troops in like this. Don't you know?"

Solo turned a rueful smile on his new-found ally.

"I work for a man who sends me on errands and then explains to me exactly what I went for after I get back. But I have some ideas. Fromes was a friend of mine and I know what interested him more than anything else on earth. Chemical warfare."

She shuddered again. He idly wondered what kind of figure the leather jacket and whipcord breeches contained. It was hard to tell in the gloom of the cabin.

"Now, the sixty-four thousand dollar question," he prodded.

"All right."

"You have pinpointed me exactly—to the dot and stroke of the clock. How did you know I was coming to Rouen to rent this plane?"

She showed him the white teeth again.

"We have our own methods, Watson."

"You'll have to do better than quoting Sherlock Holmes. I need some proof you are who you say you are—besides your dazzling smile. Give."

"What will you do if I don't?" she challenged.

"I can kill you without leaving a trace."

Her eyes met his and something stirred, on the female side, in their dark brown depths.

"I'll just bet you could. Fair enough. We knew you were at the Internationale, you were followed to Le Bourget when you left. And a certain Mr. X is a fairly close friend of your Overseas Club contact. Get the picture? One top echelon man tells another top echelon man and the agents fend for themselves."

He nodded. "I'm convinced."

"Thank you."

"What are your plans for Oberteisendorf? I don't intend to saw Stewart Fromes' body in half just to make friends with Army Intelligence."

It was a grim joke to get a laugh out of her and he respected her for not even smiling.

"No. I simply wish to be with you when you claim the body. And to look around. Then we part company. We want U.N.C.L.E. to have the body."

"That's white of you."

She sensed the bitterness in his voice. "Was he a very good friend of yours?"

"The best kind. Never changed colors or patterns on you."

"I'm very sorry, then."

"Don't be." He was abrupt and curt. He saw the sudden flush in her cheeks and immediately felt sorry. He changed the subject again as a sudden thought came to him.

"Can we land anywhere near Oberteisendorf?"

She nodded. "We checked out the terrain. There's a five hundred acre meadow to the south of the town. One problem though—how did you intend to get Fromes' body out of there?"

He frowned slightly. "That's what bothers me the most. Train is my only bet until I can find a plane. My plans haven't covered that yet. I expect to get some instructions tomorrow."

The Debonair droned on, a tiny dot in the dark seas of the French skies.

"Well, Kuryakin?"

Waverly stared glumly at Illya Nickovetch Kuryakin, marveling for the nth time at what fortune had guided U.N.C.L.E. to draw this man from behind the Iron Curtain. It was necessary at times to operate in that part of the world and Kuryakin had proven his merits more than once. For all of his Russian origin, the man was an excellent U.N.C.L.E. agent. Clever, resourceful, physically adept—and an excellent man in the laboratories too. Even now he was justifying Waverly's firm belief in his ability.

Illya Nickovetch Kuryakin, his thatch of straw-colored

hair awry, held up the test tube which had prompted
Waverly's attention.

"Yes, Mr. Waverly. A positive, I'm afraid."

"Hmm." Waverly turned to hide his chagrin, fumbling
for one of his pipes. "No mistake?"

"None. This sample matches the one we examined.
Therefore, both corpses were suffering from the same
disease."

"Well, that's a nice kettle of fish, I must say." He flung
a reproachful glance at Kuryakin, as if he were evidenc-
ing his usual disapproval of the Russian's rumpled suit
and sloppy tie. Kuryakin shrugged.

"When Solo returns with his body, we can run another
test. If it turns out the same way, there can be no mistake."

"Yes, yes. That's true."

Waverly worried his corncob pipe. It was a damnable
business all around. If Thrush had succeeded with the
nasty business as he well suspected, there would indeed
be hell to pay. But he had to respect Kuryakin's results.
If the blood specimens of the corpses from Utangaville,
Africa and Spayerwood, Scotland, showed the same X
factor, why then, the proof was there. Of what, he did
not know—save that his research laboratory experts had
found one exact, unknown similarity between both blood
specimens. Something they vouched could not happen
in one hundred million attempts.

"Have you heard from Solo yet, Mr. Waverly?"

"No. But I intend to phone him transatlantic, twelve
o'clock Germany time. Tomorrow. He should be where
he's supposed to be by then."

"If anyone can make an appointment at the right time
he can."

"Hmm. Indeed. Well, Kuryakin. We'll discuss this at another time."

"Yes, Sir."

Back at his quiet desk, with the row of enamel buttons, the head of Section I, U.N.C.L.E. found a neatly stacked mass of reports awaiting him. The teletype and recorder machines had issued forth a harvest of data. It was Waverly's daily duty to keep abreast of all that happened in the world as it affected the organization.

Waverly put away his corncob and attacked the pile.

Yet even as his mind flew over the data, absorbing the material therein, he couldn't shake a gloomy feeling of impending doom in the pit of his ancient stomach.

The reports on the Le Bourget fire and the hullaballoo at the Hotel Internationale had had a demoralizing effect on him.

He seemed to have sent Napoleon Solo on an assignment which did nothing but raise a swarm of hornets.

Damnation, he thought.

It only went to prove that Stewart Fromes' corpse was of the utmost importance to someone. Yet, why consent to turn a man's body over to his friends if you meant to do nothing but keep the friends from obtaining that body?

A puzzler, indeed. And for a man whose lifelong passion was a good game of chess, a dazzling problem.

Waverly's eyes suddenly glowed and the reports fell away beneath him. His dour face almost broke into a full smile.

Of course. The very thing! The only reason, the single possible motive for such a play. Why hadn't he thought of it sooner?

Swiftly, his thumb reached for the row of buttons. He poked the yellow buzzer this time.

The metallic voice clicked on:

"Yes, Mr. Waverly?"

"Get me the War Room in the Pentagon. The Joint Chiefs of Staff. I wish to talk to the head of the Army Air Force."

"Hold on, Sir."

Waverly, in his eagerness to explore his new-found theory and impatient to put his plan into operation, explored the center drawer of his desk until he produced a regulation briar pipe. He sucked on it briefly, tapped the bowl with a stiff finger and waited.

His eyes still held the look of a man who had stumbled on a great truth.

When the call went through and the voice of the head of the Army Air Force came over the wire, Waverly plunged into his request.

U.N.C.L.E., it seemed, had immediate top priority use for a jet bomber flight to Paris, without payload, to connect Waverly with an Air-Sea Rescue helicopter for a pickup in Oberteisendorf, Germany.

Meanwhile, over four thousand miles away, Napoleon Solo's Beechcraft Debonair was setting down in the very early morning darkness that closed like a shroud over the sleeping town of Oberteisendorf, Germany.

A COFFIN FOR U.N.C.L.E.

THE FUNERAL parlor which contained Stewart Fromes'
body was a living mockery. It was hard to believe that
Oberteisendorf was even a town of any size. In the darkness of landing at night, which Solo had done expertly and with fine command of the patch of ground
left for the job, the town had seemed little more than
several rows of houses divided by a running stream of
water which flowed steadily under a joke of a bridge.
Once they had quit the vicinity of the plane, Napoleon
Solo had known where to go.

Every German town or village has a *Burgomeister*,
or Mayor. They found Herr Burgomeister's dwelling on
the main street of the town, with a hanging oaken sign
suspended from cast-iron moorings which proclaimed
the information: BURGOMEISTER.

Napoleon Solo had roused that irate individual from
a sound sleep, banging loudly on the front door. A frightened *hausfrau* had peeked down owlishly from a shut-
tered window, then hurried to fetch her husband. While
they waited on the rutted road below, Solo had taken
stock of a few things. He was worn to the bone, and
starved—and Geraldine Terry had a splendid figure.
She was nearly as tall as he but her chest measurements
were far more satisfactory and in shapelier evidence.
The leather flying jacket now could not conceal the
surge of a ripe, womanly body.

The Burgomeister, thin and scrawny and old, gawked in relief when Solo flashed his impressive U.N.C.L.E. credentials, which to the world at large was some kind of charitable organization for the needy and underprivileged. It was so easy for the casual observer to assume from Solo's outer appearance that he was some wealthy young man who had decided to be a philanthropist as his life's work.

Herr Muller was impressed, too.

"*Ja.* I glad you come. 'Bout time you take your friend."

"I've made good time, all things considered."

"*Ja, ja.* Is true. But one day too long and we have to bury your friend."

"I don't understand—"

"Do not misunderstand. He was fine man. But law here, body must be claimed by two days or we must bury body. You understand—he rot and smell if we don't. No how do you call it—facilities for refrigeration."

"Please take us to him now, Herr Muller."

The undertaker's parlor was no more than a squat, ugly brown building of stone and wood. Inside, a dim bulb burned feebly. Solo reflected bitterly that the undertaker's calling was the same the world over. Keep a light burning in the window all day long to remind the living that someday they must die so now was the time to make plans—

Stewart Fromes' corpse lay on a flat wooden table, a long sheet of gray muslin draped over his entire length. There was a faint yet already palpable odor of decay in the room. Solo frowned, motioning Jerry Terry to stay back as he came forward. He moved toward the sheet. Upstairs, he could hear the mortician, who had remained out of sight, exchanging guttural German insults with the Burgomeister.

Solo, face expressionless, removed the sheet from Stewart Fromes' body.

It was not easy to look at. Stewart Fromes' corpse was a scene from Hell.

His exposed face had already begun to rot, the first signs of visible decay baring the cartilage of his nose and laying back the gums of his mouth. Flesh lay thin and decomposing on the lean face that Solo had known so well. Solo's insides revolted; his logic reeled.

Stewart Fromes looked like he had been dead for a month. There was no denying the utter gauntness and yellowing, rotting dead tissues of his face. The features had all withdrawn to resemble the wrinkled, leathery-dry rot of decay.

Yet, with all the horror of the situation and the revelation, there was one more staggering blow to sanity.

Stewart Fromes' clothes were all *reversed*.

It was as unmistakable as the condition of the dead man's face.

His jacket was on backwards, straitjacket style. His shirt was the same peculiar way, showing the rear of the collar as if he were a minister. There was no tie, naturally. Solo, still revolted, bent to examine the corpse. Stewart Fromes' trousers were on backwards too.

The only place where the motif had been ignored was the feet. Stewart Fromes' ten stiff naked toes wore no shoes.

Napoleon Solo stepped back, completely baffled. This was like some double blasphemy of the dead. Like some filthy joke that had no point other than shame and unholy mortification. He felt anger begin to cloud his reason. He shook it off. There was overtly something devilishly remarkable about the whole thing.

Stewart Fromes looked as though there would not be a single mark on his body to indicate what had killed him. Yet his body was rotting away before Solo's very eyes and all of his apparel had been reversed. Why, in God's name?

"Napoleon," Jerry Terry shuddered. "What does it mean?"

"I don't know. Let's just wait until our German friends are done with their bickering. I've never run up against anything like this before."

Herr Burgomeister bobbed into view, his scrawny figure agitated. "That fool Klingeheim. He lost a little sleep—" He paused, bewildered. He had seen the look in Napoleon Solo's eye.

"*Bitte*, is something wrong?"

"Yes, Herr Muller. I find my friend's body badly taken care of. And his clothes most unusually arranged."

"Please," the Burgomeister begged. "We have no facilities! I am sorry, you must know that. As for his clothes —we find him like this. In the kitchen of his house. I swear. We touch nothing."

"You're sure?"

"*Ja, ja.* I swear."

"Where is his laboratory, please?"

"Two squares over. Come. You are done here?"

"No, I will come back to guard the body. And I'll need ice. Lots of ice. You understand? The body must be kept from decomposing further before I can return it to America. Tell your Mr. Klingenheim I want a coffin. I'll pay him well. Can you do these things for me?"

"Ye-e-es—"

"Good. I want nothing touched. I will crate the body myself. Is that understood now, Herr Muller?"

The commands were so evenly stated, so unequivocally pronounced that even if Herr Muller knew little of this Napoleon Solo, he knew him well enough now to be afraid.

"Do you take me for a dumbkopf, Herr Solo? I do. I do."

"Fine. Now show me where my friend stayed in Oberteisendorf."

The Burgomeister led the way, clucking fearfully, guiding them with a swinging hurricane lamp which splattered yellowish rays over the sickly landscape. Jerry Terry clung to Solo's right arm and huddled close to him as they walked.

It was a small, cottage-like place set further back than the homes flanking its low sides. The paint was peeling and ugly black patches shone through the cornices of the structure. Herr Muller ushered them to the front door, and shrugged his shoulders in resignation, before he turned away to do Solo's bidding in the matter of the corpse.

"Oh, Herr Muller," Solo called before he had darted from view.

"*Bitte?*"

"Where is Frau Morgernstern? The lady who was his housekeeper."

"Gone. Run away. Have not seen her since the terrible thing. No one see her."

With that, he was gone.

Jerry Terry shivered. "This is an ugly little town. I feel it in my bones."

"I agree wholeheartedly with your bones. Come on in. And watch out for low-flying bats."

There was a light switch close to the front door. Oberteisendorf had electricity, at least—it wasn't as backwards as all that. Perhaps it might even seem liveably decent in the daylight.

Stewart Fromes' home away from home was a modest two-room affair with loft above. This he had converted into his laboratory. Solo lit a cigarette and loosened his tie. The plain, simple furniture mocked him.

"Okay, Memory Girl. Let's go over the complete set-up. Top to bottom. If there's anything at all here we should know about, let's find it. Stewart Fromes is not going to go to waste. Not if we can help it. Right?"

"Right."

Side by side, they worked through the two rooms, emptying everything, overturning all in sight. Solo even drained a sugar bowl and coffee pot, sifting the dead grounds for clues. Nothing. The place was as devoid of personal belongings as a hotel room can be.

"See anything, Jerry?"

"Nothing. Shall we try the loft?"

"Yes. That was his real home. He would have left his imprint there more than anywhere."

Yet, twenty minutes later, Napoleon Solo admitted to defeat. He felt completely stymied. Beyond finding the same old Bunsen Burners, slides and scientific apparatus, a research chemist might need, he was absolutely in the dark. What was worse, they had not even stumbled upon a book of notes or records or some such daily log in which to record data.

"Blind alley, Solo?"

"Maybe, Terry. But I don't think so. He had notes all right—lots of them. In his head and on paper. Trouble is, whoever killed him forgot nothing. They got the notes too."

"That would make sense—if he found something."

He must have," Solo said, "or he wouldn't have been killed."

She sighed. "We don't know for a fact that he was killed."

He stared at her. "The high altitude must have scrambled your brains, Miss Terry. Agents like Stewart Fromes just don't keel over in mid-day because they have high blood pressure."

"Probably not. But I wish we knew for sure."

Solo cast a last long mournful look about the house. He shook his head, fatigue making his voice as raspy as a file.

"He found out something all right. Right here and right in this room. And they found out about *him*, so killed him—in a way that's caused his body to start decomposing immediately." Solo paused frowning. "I wish we knew what we were looking for so we'd know what it was when we found it."

She smiled wanly. "I'll bet you can't say that all over again, Mr. Solo, and get it perfectly straight."

"I'll tell you something. I'm not even going to try." He took her arm. "Come on, lady, tough work ahead yet. You have to help me pack a coffin."

He felt her body stiffen beside him. Their eyes locked. "Do I have to—Napoleon?"

"No, of course you don't. But it will be easier if you help."

"Then I'll help," she said.

He kissed her quickly, full on the mouth, and drew back before she could either slap him or respond. Her eyes had widened in surprise.

He laughed. "You thought I was going to make love to you right here and now?"

"Something like that," she confessed.

"Something like that," Solo smiled, "will come later. I promise you."

They marched, hand in hand, back to the mortician's parlor, with sleeping Oberteisendorf closing them in on all sides and the dark sky above. Jerry Terry yawned sleepily. Napoleon Solo fought to keep his eyes open. It had been a very long night.

It wasn't over yet, either.

At the far end of the village, just where the last house disappeared under a shelving of trees, Herr Muller rapped at a wooden door. He was admitted quickly by a tall, lanky man nearly a head higher. The Burgomeister held his hat fearfully between his thin fingers, alternately crumbling and pulling it apart.

It was a small, bare room. Only an upended barrel with a single wax candle set on it provided illumination.

The tall man stood behind the light, his face in the shadows, his figure looming large on the ceiling. His body was encased in something that was more than cape and less than cloak.

"Report," the tall man said in a low voice. It was hollow and somehow unreal, like something heard in a vault.

"A man come. For the body."

"What man?"

"Solo. Mr. Solo. A real *Herr*."

"Alone?"

"No. Woman with him. Lovely *maedchen*."

The tall man heaved a curse across the room. The candle flickered as if it might expire. Thin Herr Muller nearly jumped in his fright.

"What does Herr Solo demand of you?"

"Coffin. Ice. Much ice. He wants to prevent body from more decomposing."

"So." The tall man laughed, briefly and chillingly. "Anything else?"

"*Nein. Bitte*, that was all he ask."

The tall man laughed.

"Good. Give him his coffin. Give him his ice. Obey all he tells you."

"*Bitte—*"

"Go now. That will be all."

Herr Muller nodded, his throat working nervously. Turning, he fairly crawled out of sight. The door closed softly behind him. The tall man moved to the candle, bent over it to extinguish the flame.

Briefly, the light illuminated a face from hell.

Then the flame puffed out and the room was once more in darkness.

THE BADLY-DRESSED CORPSE

"WHAT ARE YOU thinking about now, Solo?"

"The same thing you must be."

"The corpse?"

"Yes. Any other time I would be thinking of you. But Stew's corpse was enough to throw me into a tailspin. The fantastically quick decomposition . . . and the clothes. They were to mean something. He isn't dressed that way because he was an eccentric."

They were sitting quietly in the parlor of Herr Muller's home, enjoying the solitude of each other's company and a blissful cigarette. The smoke filled the air with lazy spirals of unbroken perfection until they collided with the beamed ceiling. Like most rural German homes, the Burgomeister's house was mostly wooden.

Solo had had a frantic two hours upon their return from Stewart Fromes' place. There had been the matter of the coffin. A cheap pine box, shaped nearly like a mummy case. With the mortician's help and Jerry Terry's aid, they had placed Steward Fromes in the coffin. Finally, they had secured enough ice to defer further decomposition for a few more hours. Solo had found some plastic bags in Fromes' workshop which served. He had nothing more to do with the corpse other than to examine the reversed clothes. But there was nothing immediately apparent. No messages, no scraps of paper, no clues. Yet he knew for a fact that back in the

U.N.C.L.E. laboratory something would be uncovered. Perhaps Stewart had treated his clothes with fluorescent materials or chemicals which would turn up under black light. It couldn't end like this. Thrush hadn't dressed him that way to be found by his friends. They weren't in the business of leaving clues. No—the clothes had been Stew's idea. Why?

Napoleon Solo didn't know.

All he experienced now was a vast weariness of brain, limb and soul. He blinked across the room at Jerry Terry.

She was smiling at him. "If you want to talk I'll listen. We should both be tucked in our beds but you look like a man who can't sleep—too much thinking to do."

"Something like that," he admitted.

"Any ideas?"

He puffed on the cigarette. "A few. The kind of things you have to drum up when you're in the dark. I'm thinking about Stewart Fromes. What kind of a man he was—whatever I can remember about him. It's screwy but I suddenly realize a lot of water has gone over the dam and we didn't have much of a chance to get friendlier."

"What was he like?" she asked softly.

"Brilliant. Won a medal in Korea. Majored in Chemistry at Cornell, came out near the head of his class. He'd been with U.N.C.L.E. for nearly ten years. He was a bachelor, though he was almost hooked by a Hollywood actress once. That was his broken-heart period. He liked the Yankees, was a good golfer and—" Solo sat up, his eyes narrowing—"was an inveterate reader of mystery novels. Everything and anything. Fact is, we used to kid him about it."

"You've thought of something?"

"Maybe."

"Something constructive?"

It was odd, but the spurring softness of her voice filtering across the quiet room helped immensely. She was a sounding board for any and all ideas he might come up with—even crazy ones.

"I think so. But I'll have to sleep on it."

She laughed lightly. "That's a good one. Sleep where? The Burgomeister has no extra beds. I imagine these chairs are it for the rest of the night."

He looked toward the windows. A dull glow of approaching dawn made the squared area ghostly.

"German hospitality still has a Nazi flavor in some ares, I suppose. Just as well. You never know when you're shaking hands with a man who stood by those ovens. It's a creepy sensation. This chair will do me fine."

"Napoleon—"

"I'm still here."

She had left her chair to glide softly across the room. She was before him in an instant. A beautiful pixie with coppery hair and hauntingly lovely face. The crude lamps of the parlor made her face glow like some bronze Goddess. She put her hands to his cheeks, bent and kissed him swiftly on the lips.

"We're even now," she whispered.

"New breed, huh?"

Her eyes narrowed. "Just what does *that* mean?"

"Well, you see what you want and you take it. I'm all for new breeds. Can't tell. A little judicious mating and future generations may turn out not half bad—"

She was starting to get angry, color mounting in her

cheeks. His bantering manner caused her to push away, averting her face. Solo laughed, reached out and pulled her back. He held her tightly so that her body was crushed against his own in the narrow confines of the chair. She squirmed, trying to get away from him, but he held her easily, almost as though she were a child.

He turned her around to face him, and said, "I really did mean that as a compliment, you know. If it didn't sound completely serious, that's only because of a peculiar quirk of mine—too many people I like have ended up dead, so I try not to take important things seriously anymore."

"You're a stinker," she murmured, all the fight gone out of her.

"Takes one to know one, doesn't it, Miss Terry?"

The chair was not the best place in the world to discover suddenly that they liked each other very much.

But they managed.

The utter stillness of the morning was staggering in its quietude. For a metropolitan man used to the throb and roar of big cities and thundering sidewalks, it proved a genuine soporific. Napoleon Solo had to be awakened.

He opened his eyes to see Jerry Terry's lovely smile just inches from his eye.

"We have bacon and eggs," she said happily. "Come on. Coffee's on the boil and the good Mullers, both him and her, are off to City Hall to see about arrangements for getting us out of here."

He sat up, rubbing his eyes and running fingers through his sleep-mussed hair.

Abruptly, the girl said, "Is Napoleon your real name?"

He pretended to be hurt. "Don't you like it?"

"I love it. I simply noticed that you have the Bonaparte hairdo. That dark little forelock that dangles on your forehead."

"I'll cut it off," he promised.

"You do and I'll never talk to you again," she vowed. "Come on. There's a Civil War sink in the kitchen."

The light, flippant talk was good. It helped drive away the worries, doubts and fears. The food was even better. Herr Burgomeister had a stocked larder that in another period of history would have made him suspected of Black Market affiliations.

Jerry Terry bustled around the kitchen, setting plates and pouring coffee with all the animated enthusiasm of a new bride. Solo smiled in memory. The analogy would serve. The first time was always somehow, the best time. It had an aura of magic all its own.

"More coffee?"

"Please. Dare I hope there's a wireless office in town? Strikes me I'd better get in touch with my people."

"All you can do is ask Mr. Muller when he gets back."

"Did you notice a railroad when we flew in last night?"

She shook her head. "It's hard to tell from that altitude. Especially at night. But there has to be one around somewhere."

He smiled grimly. "That ice won't last forever. We have to do something, and quick. Unless our Mr. Waverly has a few rabbits up his sleeve."

"Mr. Waverly?"

"My section chief. I'm sure he's thought of something. What time do you have?" He checked his own wrist watch.

"Eleven fifteen."

"Same here. Our watches are synchronized. Now, I'll finish this coffee and we'll shoot over to see about Fromes and that cablegram I have to send. Failing that, the phone is my next best bet."

The coffin was secure on the wooden table where they had left it. Ignoring the cackling mortician who was asking in broken English what it was all about, Solo lifted the lid and re-examined Stewart Fromes.

The mixture was as before. The dead chemist looked as ghastly as before and his clothes still remained in their peculiar fixed reversal of the norm. It was uncanny. Fortunately, the ice seemed to have helped. The unpleasant odor of death was somewhat subdued.

"Jerry," Solo said, without turning. "Would you ask the Herr Mortician to point out the direction of the cable office? Or someplace where we can use a phone?"

She caught on quickly. Within seconds, she had charmed the old man from the room. Solo bent quickly over Stewart Fromes and made a closer survey than he had the night before.

The hands were hopelessly stiff. The decaying process was working fast. Fromes had worn no rings and his fingers were empty. His throat was free of pendants, lockets or identification disks of any kind. Solo worked quickly down the length of the body to the naked feet. It was there that he took his greatest effort. One by one, he pried the locked toes apart. It was gruesome work. Fromes' flesh felt flacid and loose, as if it would come apart at the touch of a finger.

Stewart Fromes had large feet but he had managed to keep them clean and fairly uncalloused. The toenails were in excellent condition. But between his fourth and little toe on the right foot, Napoleon Solo found the one item he was looking for. It was a repellant task but it had to be done.

A silver pellet, looking as innocuous as a B-B shot, fell into his palm. He held it up to the light, revolving it, his eyebrows knit in fierce concentration.

Here again was an intangible.

Had the pellet accidentally wedged itself between the corpse's toes at some time prior to death? Had it been placed there to be found? By whom? Fromes . . . the enemy—or who?

There was no more time to guess. Jerry Terry was coming back, the mortician in tow, with Herr Muller bouncing excitedly behind them. The scrawny Burgomeister looked unhappy about something.

Napoleon Solo arched his eyebrows.

"Solo," Jerry Terry said, "there are merely three telephones in this thriving little town. Two are unavailable to us now because the people are away and Herr Burgomeister says his phone is on the blink. As for places where one can send telegrams—" She shook her head in sad negation.

"That's nice," he said, pinning the Burgomeister with a look. "Where is the nearest place where we can contact civilization?"

Herr Muller forced an apologetic smile and held up his ten thin fingers.

"Ten kilometers. Bad Winzberg. I get car—truck. Drive you."

"That's good to know. Let me think a minute. There must be some better way—"

"The plane?" Jerry Terry asked.

He shook his head. "It wasn't meant to ferry coffins. We can't have Stew banging around like a load of apples. No, there has to be a better way. And I must contact my people—"

Herr Muller's eyes took on a crafty gleam.

"You bury here. Why not? Fine cemetery. Later you dig up, re-bury in America, *nicht yahr?*"

Solo hesitated, visibly.

"What cemetery?"

Herr Muller's eyes widened in pride.

"You don't know? Orangeberg. Biggest cemetery in all this part of country. Back in wartime was left by Allies. Three, maybe four hundred dead there. Not far. We reach there in half hour from here. Close to Black Forest."

"You mean a cemetery for American soldiers. War memorial?" Solo had never heard of one in this part of the world, but then, he had not heard of everything.

"*Nein, nein,*" Herr Muller protested, with the mortician adding his gutturals to the chorus. "Our cemetery. For our people. Very nice there. You see. Like, like—" He searched for a proper word. "Like your Arlington in America!"

Jerry Terry looked at Napoleon Solo. Her face was faintly bemused but her eyes held refusal.

"Thanks for the offer, Herr Muller. But it's no dice. I must take my friend back to the States. And right away. Now, if you'll see about that truck, we'll get him ready."

Herr Muller was pained. "You will not reconsider—"

"Sorry. No."

"But, but—"

The spluttering of Herr Muller was suddenly drowned

out in the mammoth roar of a motor directly overhead —a thundering, blasting boom of sound which seemed to make the four walls of the mortuary rattle. A dish fell somewhere and a tin cup clattered. Jerry Terry shouted with pleasure as Solo raced to the doorway for a look.

High overhead, he could see the briskly clawing giant helicopter as it climbed quickly over the rooftops of the town. There was no mistaking the circling pattern of the flight. Solo stood and watched, smiling widely as he made out the American insignia and markings of the Air-Sea Rescue. By God, he would get Stewart Fromes home after all.

"Mr. Waverly," he muttered feelingly, "thank you, very much."

DEATH FOR THE DEBONAIR

STEWART FROMES' corpse was on its way back to the States. It would be delivered to U.N.C.L.E. Headquarters and then placed in the laboratory where a team of experts would try to determine what had killed him. There was no more worry about that.

Solo was not too surprised that Mr. Waverly had decided to come along for the helicopter ride. The old warhorse was like that. Indeed, on many of Solo's hazardous ventures for U.N.C.L.E. Mr. Waverly had shown up in the damnedest places at the damnedest times.

Looking at him now, in the Burgomeister's office, Solo found it hard to believe that the old man was as stonily impatient with him as he eternally seemed. Waverly always made him feel like a pet student who had somehow failed to get 100 on a written examination in Strategy despite all of Waverly's sound teachings. Jerry Terry had gone to see about the Debonair, dependent on the outcome of Solo's interview with his Chief. Oberteisendorf, of course, was agog, having seen little activity since the days when armored task forces had roared through the town.

Now, aircraft had thundered overhead and officials of that big powerful country the United States were everywhere in evidence. Something to do with that American, the *Herr* Fromes, who had fallen down dead only two days ago—

"Well, Solo. I'm sure you have much to report."

"Where should I start, Mr. Waverly?"

"Genesis, Solo. Even the Bible began there."

Solo told all he had to tell, dating from the time of his encounter with Denise Fairmount and the infernal maser device. He was certain Waverly knew all about that, but he had to be thorough. He spent some time on Stewart Fromes' peculiar condition of death as well as apparel.

When he came to the matter of the small silver pellet, Solo explained that all he could tell him about it was on the negative side. "It's not a toxic substance, and it isn't radioactive. According to all I've been able to discover in the short time I've been able to devote to it, it seems to be harmless. However, there's undoubtedly more here than meets the eye—*or* the geiger counter. A matter for the laboratory, I'd say."

The old man, nodding as if to himself, took the pellet and tucked it carefully into the pocket of his vest. His baggy, wrinkled tweeds and thoughtful frown matched perfectly. This time, however, he seemed to have left his pipes behind in New York.

"You could fill me in a little, Mr. Waverly."

"Yes, I suppose I could. But before we return to Fromes' curious case, I would like to tell you that the Fairmount woman is definitely a Thrush agent. Our file on her is most extensive. Oddly enough, Fairmount is her real name. She uses it on special occasions. It is interesting that they wanted to sacrifice her when they employed the maser device. I must confess to no surprise at its existence. It has been employed once before, against an Israeli scientist. The poor fellow was driven out of his mind. But I don't think they have managed yet to lick the problem altogether. There seem to be a few bugs in the thing, still."

Solo nodded. "Then you don't imagine Thrush has worked it into a large-scale weapon?"

Waverly pursed his lips. "Time enough for that later on, but no, I do not think so. We seem to have other secret weapons to think about at this time, Solo."

"And Denise Fairmount?"

"She was not at the hotel when investigators arrived. For your information, she is a ranking Colonel in Thrush circles. Thanks to her beauty, her value has been considerable for Thrush. She also seems to be a brilliant young lady."

Solo's smile was tinged with bitterness.

"I should have killed her, then. I had her in the palm of my hand."

Waverly shrugged. "Forget her for a time. Let us now

discuss what you have just placed in the palm of *my* hand."

Solo was more than willing to forget the subject of Denise Fairmount.

"What I handed you—that little silver gizmo—that could be a Booby Trap for Booby Troops."

Waverly shook his head, smiling. "Nothing so romantic or so simple, I'm afraid. You see, Solo, I don't know how much you've learned on this assignment as relates to Fromes, but you did know why we sent him here in the first place. I'm sure your friend Kuryakin gave you some clues."

Solo nodded. "Yes, I remember. There was some idea of a powerful drug or some such that crippled whole populations, and the organization had somehow imagined that Oberteisendorf might be the next testing ground. Am I correct?"

"Partly. I'll take you back a bit. The obscure village of Utangaville and a Scottish whistle stop called Spayerwood. Last year—two months apart—one day all the people in both those tiny spots turned into completely mindless creatures. Utangaville was first, then Spayerwood. The people were incapable of speech or coherent, coordinated action. It was quite as if they had been transformed into gibbering idiots. Both towns literally died—everyone in Utangaville was dead within two days, and in Spayerwood it all happened overnight. There were three hundred and fifty natives in Utangaville. Spayerwood was practically a hamlet—ninety-seven adults and twenty-seven children. The smaller number of people there may partially account for the shorter time-period.

"It wasn't determined exactly what caused their

deaths. All sorts of notions were formed, of course. Mysterious virus, some epidemic—a plague of some kind. Yet there was nothing conclusive. The situation has not reoccurred, and everyone has breathed a trifle easier. But—" He paused meaningfully.

"You expect it to happen again."

"Decidedly. It has the mark of Thrush written all over it. For one thing, the markedly shorter amount of time it took to finish off Spayerwood—it couldn't have been *just* because there were fewer people. I'm afraid it sounds like some organization has been experimenting with and improving its methods of killing whole populations."

"Thrush, then," said Solo.

Waverly nodded. "Yes. And judging from the state of Fromes' body, they seem to be continuing their research." He paused. "Anyway, Fromes uncovered something in the lab. I'm not familiar with the terms but he claimed there was some pointed similarity between Utangaville, Spayerwood and Oberteisendorf which made him insist the trail led here. I saw no harm in assigning a fine man and excellent chemist to follow a hunch, as it were. I'm sorry it turned out this way but I'm quite certain Fromes was correct. Otherwise he would not be dead."

"With his clothes turned backwards." Solo sighed. "I hope the silver ball means something."

"It does and it will. Depend on it, Solo."

He drew out his cigarettes and extended one to Waverly without thinking. The old man demurred and Solo shook his head.

"I *am* tired. I forgot the pipe routine."

"What do you think about this rearrangement of clothing, Solo?"

"Two things, Sir. I'm positive Fromes did it as a message. He was leaving a calling card for us after death."

Waverly's eyes narrowed. "Odd you should jump to that conclusion. Wouldn't it have been simpler to leave a written message in code or some such?"

"No good, Sir. Thrush would have seen it, and would have understood it sooner or later. No, he was leaving something only we would comprehend. Don't you see? It adds up. If what you say about this drug or whatever it is is true, maybe there was no time for anything else. Maybe his last conscious act was to reverse his clothing while he was dying."

Waverly shrugged.

"You may have it, my boy. I'm not sure I can disagree with you."

Sunlight was streaming through Herr Muller's windows. Waverly blinked against the light. He looked at his watch.

"Takeoff in fifteen minutes. Well, Solo, here are your new instructions. I will return to New York with the body. The Air Force is most obliging. You will return to Paris with Miss Terry. You have wings, I understand. As soon as you settle down somewhere—may I suggest you avoid the Hotel Internationale this trip—call me and I'll let you know what we have learned about Fromes."

"You trust Miss Terry?"

"Dear boy, we must. She is all that she says she is." Waverly stood. "Clear now, as to what is to be done?"

"All the way down the line. By the way, did you ever

77

hear of a fairly large cemetery in this vicinity? Place called Orangeberg. Seems to be quite famous around these parts."

Waverly frowned. "Can't say that I have. Why do you ask?"

"Herr Muller, the Burgomeister, seemed pretty keen on my burying Stewart Fromes' body there."

"A kindness, perhaps. Never be too suspicious of everyone. It could be a bad habit to develop. You will lose your perspective."

"Could be. I'm not so sure in this case."

"You should think more, Solo, of why even a town of this size makes it difficult for you to keep a body preserved. Something strange there. But nothing to worry about now."

"No," Solo said. "Thanks to you."

Waverly glanced at his watch again. "I should say it was time I was joining the Air Force. Goodbye, Solo. See you in New York."

"Goodbye, Mr. Waverly."

Napoleon Solo stood where he was for a full five minutes after Waverly had gone. An idea had kindled in his head, only to flicker out again. It was annoying. He was certain that it had had something to do with Stewart Fromes having his clothes on backwards. Those clothes had to mean something.

Repressing his disgust, he went out to see about the plane and Jerry Terry.

They stood at the end of the meadow, watching the shining helicopter climb out of sight. The roar of its passage overhead whipped the knee-high stalks at the end of the field into a leaning pattern of graceful design.

Jerry Terry squinted in the sunlight of a warm, balmy afternoon.

"Hey, Solo," she said. "Want to go for an airplane ride?"

"I'm with you, Miss Terry. Can you fly one of these things as well as warm it up?"

"Try me. You could use the rest."

The cabin was sleek, smooth and familiar. Like an old friend. Solo locked the door on his side and settled back. His face wore a frown, however.

"What's the matter with you today, lover? You look blue."

"I'm just surprised we got out of town without any shooting going on. I usually have to blast my way out of places like Ye Olde Oberteisendorf." He indicated the throng of curious townspeople and children crowding the edge of the meadow.

She batted the ignition switch on the instrument panel.

"Forget it. My uncle is bigger than your U.N.C.L.E."

"Come again?"

"Uncle Sam, Solo. They all know we're represented by the biggest country in the world and they're impressed. Besides, the last bit of excitement around here must have been V-E Day."

"Maybe you're right. But look at Herr Muller and the mortician. They sure do look sorry to see us go."

It was true. The thin little Herr Burgomeister was positively crestfallen and the mortician reflected the same attitude. But the Debonair's motor was purring powerfully, the propellor churning briskly. Jerry Terry fiddled with the control board.

"Say goodbye to Oberteisendorf," she suggested.

"Goodbye to Oberteisendorf."

Within seconds, it was all behind them. The meadow, the startled faces, the huddled ugly town. The Bavarian Alps raised snowy heads on the Eastern horizon. Jerry banked the Debonair in a gradual, even soar of speed and finally leveled off at four thousand feet. Solo stared straight ahead, thoughtfully. The sky was a floor of unbroken blue on which the Debonair skirted gracefully.

"You're still worried, Napoleon. Why?"

He sighed in exasperation. "I wish I knew why. Ever get the feeling you're leaving something behind. Like unfinished business or something you had to do but you didn't."

"You feel that way now?"

"Very much so. I feel the last thing in the world we should be doing is saying goodbye to that ugly little town. And I don't know exactly why."

She flung him a look, saw the worry in his eyes. Her bright expression softened.

"Maybe we should take a look at—"

He sat up in his seat. "Of course. Though what good it will do, I don't know. See if you can find that cemetery from the air. You may have to backtrack a bit but it ought to stand out on a day as nice as this. We can't be too far from it, either."

At his word, she had nosed the ship in a climbing turn, arrowing back in the direction they had come. Solo peered through the plexiglass, straining for the ground below. The earth from the air was a wide unending carpet, broken into terraced squares and oblongs and rectangles of all sizes and colors.

It was a mere five minutes before he saw the cemetery.

"There!" A flat expanse of earth, broken only by neat, orderly rows of stone markers.

"I'll lower down. Hang on."

The Debonair dropped like an elevator. Solo hung on, the sinking sensation in his stomach suddenly exhilarating like a roller coaster ride.

She cut her flying speed and arced the plane in a sweeping glide. The tiny squares of stone drew nearer with dizzying speed as the earth rushed up to meet them.

She leveled off, the Debonair skipping across the cemetery, yards above the earth. Solo scanned the tableau.

It was a beautiful place. Tended green landscape, flowers still in evidence. The whole area looked well cared for and arranged by a master landscape artist. That was all there was time for. The plane climbed, avoiding the wall of trees just ahead. Jerry sniffed the air.

"Cozy. Another look?"

"One more, maybe, though I don't know what the hell I'm looking for."

On the second pass, Solo tried to estimate the number of headstones. But the ground roared by and they were aloft again.

"Herr Muller was right. A lovely spot."

"Orangeberg. Nice name somehow."

"Yes." He was still trying to think of that elusive thing that was dancing around in his brain, but it was useless. He was weary and so was his mind. "I made out about two hundred headstones. Muller said there were that many at least—"

"I never flew over a cemetery before."

"You're likely to do lots of things you never did before, on this assignment."

She laughed. "Paris, next?"

"Non-stop, if you please."

The cemetery of Orangeberg moved away from them as they rose to the West. The sun was now a blinding red ball in the sky—and neither of them saw the whining black shadow which dropped from behind its concealing corona of blaze.

The dark shadow power-dived and fastened itself on their tail with deadly intent.

The next sound either Napoleon and Jerry Terry heard was the thudding, frenzied pound of .50 calibre machine-gun fire slamming into the wings of the Beechcraft Debonair.

THE WINGS OF THRUSH

JERRY TERRY said, "Oh!" and that was all. For Napoleon Solo, it said it all. Oh, indeed. The wings of the Debonair shivered and seemed to flap wide open under the withering hail of lead. And then the black shadow had shot past them into full view.

Solo's eyes opened wide as he saw the plane. It was an MIG fighter, one of those Russian destroyers he had seen in action in Korean skies. The Debonair was a go-cart compared to it. He and Jerry Terry didn't have a chance.

"Go down," he barked. "Right now. We haven't got a prayer staying up here with him. One more pass and he'll rip our wings off like cancelled stamps."

"Hang onto your breakfast," she sang out. "There's only one way out of this." He knew what she meant. Even as he scanned the skies for the MIG, he knew what she would do. He had gauged her mind and her courage well. She wasn't an Army Intelligence officer because she had nice coppery hair or good legs.

The Debonair heeled over, almost whining in protest, as she worked it into a flat spin. A dangerous maneuver but with death staring at them over the muzzle of twin .50 calibre machine guns, it was the only chance worth taking.

And the MIG had banked and roared on back at them.

Jerry Terry's quick-thinking slip down caused the fusillade of new fire to spray harmlessly across the heavens. The Debonair had one advantage—it could fall faster than the MIG could fly forward. Unless the MIG decided to follow them down. Solo bit his lip to ease the tension. He felt helpless and useless. She was doing all the work.

The Debonair dropped like a rock, the wings dancing erratically because of the gaping wounds in the metal. The pilot of the MIG barrel-rolled beautifully, shortened a pass that would have carried him miles away and hummed on back for another try. But the altitude was giving away. Another loss of five hundred feet and the MIG couldn't dare stay close.

Still, the unknown pilot had his instructions—and

cast-iron nerves. Even as the Debonair spiraled swiftly toward the ground, reaching that point of no return where Jerry would have to level off, the MIG pilot was setting itself for one last-ditch, all-out effort.

The MIG loomed in the rear-view mirror. A black phantom of unbelievable speed, shooting at them from nearly a forty-five degree angle to catch them as they passed his angle of observation.

"Brace yourself," Solo gritted. "Some more singing telegrams coming this way."

"Watch out for yourself," she snapped back.

The air came alive with the pounding of machine-gun fire. Solo cursed. This time it was for keeps. Pounds of lead found a home in the right wing. He watched it happen, too fascinated to turn away. A stitching, ripping pattern of trouble worked along the left wing to the point where it met the fuselage. Too late, he shouted a warning. Too late, he saw the wing crumple backwards, like an arm being bent at the elbow. And then came the tearing, grating song of doom. The wing buckled and flew off like a leaf in a gale wind. The Debonair flipped over on its side, throwing Solo against the girl. Flying on one wing now, the plane plummeted helplessly like a rock cast down a deep well. Jerry Terry screamed once.

Solo ignored her. The earth was rushing up at them. Time was lost now. So was letting anybody else do the thinking for him. Solo seized the stick from Jerry and pulled back.

The sky reeled over, the terrain spun in a dizzy kaleidoscope, scored with the diving whistle and whine of the Debonair.

But the reversal of direction on the stick, coupled with

the wing loss, had a nullifying effect on the power of their dive. The plane tried to climb, losing a lot of its flying speed. But the crippled wing caused a conflict of desires, aerodynamically.

Solo kept his eyes riveted to the earth. The flat ground rocketed toward them. The Debonair flipped on its side, groaned mightily and swooped back downward again in a pancaking sweep of the ground.

It was only then that Solo closed his body over the girl's and burrowed her head into the cushion of his shoulder. There was nothing left to do now but count ten and pray.

The Debonair came down with a groaning, wounded glide of erratic flight and crumbled on its landing gear.

And then came the jarring concussion of the crash.

For Solo, it was an exploding, piledriving thunder of reverberation which seemed to lift the top of his head off. The world blazed with light and the ringing of bells —and then the darkness rushed in.

Napoleon Solo's last conscious thought was that somebody had gotten pretty damn angry just because he had wanted to take a close look at the beautiful cemetery of Orangeberg.

In the jet bomber carrying Stewart Fromes' corpse back to America, Waverly sat in the forward compartment, quietly studying his report folders. His bony forehead was beaded slightly with perspiration. His hands toyed endlessly with the silver pellet Napoleon Solo had found—the little round enigma discovered between the fourth and fifth toes of a very important corpse.

The bomber soared above the choppy green Atlantic. Staring down from his window seat, Waverly could see the limitless expanse of water. Far off on the horizon, he could make out the tall funnels of an ocean liner ploughing toward France. Probably the S.S. *United States*, he thought idly. He was giving far more attention to the problem of Utangaville, Spayerwood and, possibly, Oberteisendorf.

Waverly sighed. He wished dearly for a lengthy chat with his laboratory technicians. The time lost in travel was irksome. The Air Force was extremely cooperative, thanks to the General and his top priority classification, yet there was no one on board to confide in. Thrush was no matter to discuss with pilots, bombardiers and navigators. Nor with crew chiefs, no matter how well intentioned.

He studied the silver pellet, rotating it in his strong fingers. Was this, perhaps, the answer to the problem?

He restrained a sigh. U.N.C.L.E. had its limitations, for all of its vast organizational powers. Too often, the future had to rest in the hands of a single agent—capable and highly-trained, to be sure, yet still only one man. A single human being, in the last analysis.

The range and scope of problems attacked by U.N.-C.L.E. was enormous. There was usually a sense of something international about all of the organization's activities. But, just as some of the smaller nations of the world called upon the U.N. for assistance with certain domestic problems beyond their own abilities to handle, so did U.N.C.L.E. find itself called in on occasional local situations. Anything which affected large masses of people, or which could set up a general reaction affecting other countries or forces, was a target for U.N.C.L.E.

An organization's attempt, for example, to cause the accidental firing of a missile from one friendly power onto the territory of another friendly power, in order to cause complications within the Alliance, would suffice to bring U.N.C.L.E. agents into the field. Or the vagrant wandering of a tube of germ bacilli lost from an experimental station would have U.N.C.L.E. tracking down that bottle before all hell broke loose on the international scene. Any attempt to manipulate a nation's currency values would demand U.N.C.L.E.'s immediate countermeasures.

So it was. So it had to be. Waverly had devoted his life to U.N.C.L.E.

He sighed again, recognizing the mental process he was going through as personal justification for his own existence, and reached for his pocket ballpen. Time to make notes, jot some specific memoranda that would give him a starting point once they reached New York—

"Mr. Waverly?"

He looked up to see Captain Hendryx staring down at him. The man was tall, efficient, with a pioneer look to him. One could have imagined him in buckskin and beaver cap rather than his crisp Air Force uniform.

"What is it, Captain?"

"It's the coffin, Mr. Waverly. You'd better have a look."

Waverly rose in alarm. "Out with it, man. What's wrong with the coffin?"

Captain Hendryx shook his head.

"Wish I knew for sure. But the damnedest odor is coming from it. The coffin's in the rear hold, beyond bomb bay. Sergeant Peters has been checking it every now and then—"

Through the maze of narrow passageways, with the ribs of the ship seeming like the inside of a whale in a museum, Waverly followed the Captain. The hold was a narrow, cramped space just before the tail section where stood a baffled-looking young Sergeant, poised respectfully beside the oblong box containing Stewart Fromes' body.

Waverly stooped and sniffed. An awful odor of decay was present. Waverly straightened, trying to hold back a sense of loss and defeat.

"Sergeant," he said, "raise the lid, please."

The body had been carefully packed in dry ice. Curls of cold vapor wafted up as the Sergeant raised the lid. Waverly gasped. He couldn't help himself. It was one of the few times in his well-ordered life that he didn't know quite what to say. Or think.

Captain Hendryx said, "Oh, my God!" and the young Sergeant was about to become suddenly, violently ill.

With the lid upraised, the sight was there for all to see. To give the lie to the dry ice, the time of death and the scientific mind.

Stewart Fromes' face, hands and feet were *skeletized*. His flesh had vanished, leaving the bone-white, dull gleam of his skeletal figure. It was unearthly, it was weird—it was impossible.

It was a condition which no mere two days could have brought about. The sight was awesome and terrifying. The corpse's teeth were bared, the hollow eyes staring sightlessly up at the men surrounding the coffin.

"Close the lid, will you, Sergeant?" Waverly said calmly. "There's nothing that we can do now."

"Shakespeare," Waverly reminded Illya Nickovetch Kuryakin in U.N.C.L.E. Headquarters. "I kept being hoisted on Hamlet's line. Act Two, wasn't it?"

"Hamlet?" Kuryakin looked puzzled.

"Yes, Hamlet, man. What was the line—about Yorick —'*how long will a man's body lie in the ground ere it rot?*'"

Kuryakin nodded. "Yes. I see what you mean. Only rotting isn't the thing now, is it? We have a skeleton to contend with."

Waverly grunted, his smile blank.

"Well, it's your department. What's the answer?"

The Russian pursed his lips thoughtfully and considered his reply for a few well-chosen seconds before answering.

"I can't tell you exactly how rapidly decomposition works—that could only be determined by where the body was buried, under what conditions and just how long the interment continued—but I can tell you one thing. It certainly is a far greater period of time than three days. More like two months."

"Exactly. And that is the condition of Fromes' body on Sunday when he only died on Friday of the same week."

"We're working on it, Sir. We need just a bit more time."

"And Solo's pellet? What of that?"

Kuryakin frowned. "It's not just a pellet, we've found. It's actually a capsule—inside is a chemical substance which we're analyzing now. Every available researcher in Section II is on it—we'll have a report within hours."

"Hmmm." Waverly selected another briar from his desk drawer. "And Solo. Any word yet from Paris?"

"Nothing on the teletype. No cablegrams, no transatlantic phone calls. Which is not like him."

"No, it isn't." Waverly consulted his watch. It had been a mere three hours since the jet bomber had set down on the La Guardia runway. Time and more than time. U.N.C.L.E. should have heard from Solo hours ago. He would have reached Paris long before Hendryx landed in New York. After all, they had had an entire ocean to contend with.

Perhaps the girl—no, that couldn't be. She had checked out thoroughly with Security. Damnation. Things were getting a bit thick.

"Sir?"

"Yes, Kuryakin?"

"When we finish analyzing the chemical in the pellet, I'd like to go to Paris."

"Oh? Why, may I ask?"

"He might need a hand."

"He has one. Two, in fact. Two very pretty ones."

Illya Nickovetch Kuryakin grinned. It made him seem more harmless than ever, his straw hair untidily youthful

"Three agents are better than two."

"You are needed here, Kuryakin. But we shall see. Time enough to decide when we clear up these lab matters."

"Peculiar about Fromes' clothing, Sir. It must mean something."

Waverly smiled. "You too, eh? Perhaps you and Solo are correct. It *is* odd to find a body dressed that way."

"Any ideas?"

"A few. None that would interest you right now. If you'll be good enough to return to your office, I shall make some inquiries about our dear Solo."

"Yes, of course. Goodbye, Sir."

When Kuryakin had gone. Waverly put a few well-oiled wheels of communication into motion. Within twenty minutes he would know if Napoleon Solo had returned to Paris.

It was damned worrisome that the young idiot hadn't gotten through to Headquarters as yet.

The frightened people of Oberteisendorf had another mystery on their hands. The afternoon sky had been full of the angry, violent buzzing of two airplanes in a battle of some kind.

They had seen the fall of the lighter plane and the frenzied attack of the black one. Then the awful crash that made the ground shudder. The most ambitious and adventurous of the townspeople, a blacksmith named Goethal, set out in his battered truck for the scene of the crash. He was certain the plane had fallen somewhere in the vicinity of Orangeberg Cemetery.

When he returned two hours later, he had a grim report to make.

Yes, it was the plane that the American had come in. Yes, the plane was a mass of twisted wreckage.

No, he had not found the bodies of either of the Americans.

It was as if the earth had swallowed them up.

TWO MORE UNFORTUNATES

NAPOLEON SOLO had a dream.

In the dream he experienced no pain or pleasure, only a kind of concentrated euphoria. He was weightless, bodiless, airborne—in an existence which through vague distortions told him somehow that he was dreaming, that all he saw and did was in no way the slightest bit real.

Jerry Terry was in the dream, too.

He saw her as he had never seen her before. She was resplendently free and completely naked. The sight would normally have delighted him, yet for some reason, in his dream, it did not. Instead, it was somehow alarming, sinister. He fought to clear his head.

She was crouched before him huddled like some shapely question mark of damp, quivering flesh. Her long, slender arms were encircled with cuffs of some leathery kind. All of her superb figure was taut and stiff with her face lowered to the ground. Behind her, close to her naked flesh, he could make out a curious lattice of bars or rungs of some kind. With a sudden start, he realized, or rather he sensed, that the bars and rungs were before her now. He watched, through a haze, as she crouched and knelt, not standing erect or moving to any degree. It was quite as if she were frozen into this clumsy position of obsequiosness, as though she were humbling herself before some ancient idol.

He could see that the terrible position had cost her. Her rib cage was drawn taut, showing muscular hollows, thrusting her fine breasts into a painful cramp of beauty. The long, coppery hair had fallen limply athwart her shoulders, dangling like the rest of her. Her thighs shone with perspiration. He could hear the sketchy, impure sound of her breathing.

The walls surrounding her were ladders of bars, crossed and criss-crossed. Damp stone gleamed from a wall behind her. Somewhere not far off, he could hear the mossy mutterings of drops of liquid. Water, perhaps.

Solo blinked his eyes. It was ridiculous but—there it was. And it would not go away or shimmer into unreality like a dream.

She was still half-bent and stooped in that terrible position when he re-focussed his eyes. And now he sought to determine his own place in the scheme of his dream, or his nightmare.

He tried to stare down at himself.

He was hardly surprised to find that he too was naked; that he too was staring at his own knee-caps, performing the same weird ballet as was Jerry Terry. His own lithe body of a hundred and eighty pounds was contorted and doubled like some fantastic pretzel not of his own making.

The trouble was, he felt no pain as yet. The euphoria of his dream had not worn off.

And dream or not—he and the girl were each and separately imprisoned like some strange species of bird in awesome cages of iron. Cages large enough to hold their bodies but not big enough to permit them to stand or lie down, and so constructed that they couldn't even maneuver into a sitting position.

There were leather thongs on his wrists, holding him away from the iron lattice surrounding him. Why?

He tried to think about the Debonair.

He could remember the MIG, the big round holes in the wings and the dizzying spin into nowhere. It was all so hazy. What had happened, really? Was he dreaming or was he dead? Was this reality or simply hell? Himself—who had always loved the ladies—staked out naked in an oval cage while the loveliest lady of his immediate acquaintance was similarly indisposed a scant but inaccessible few feet away. He laughed harshly but he did not hear the sound of his own laughter. If this was Hell, they had indeed picked the right one for him.

Why didn't he feel pain? Surely, the leather thongs had bitten deep into his flesh. And the muscles of his body should be racked and spent from the ordeal. Instead, he felt simply puffy and lifeless, like a wad of absorbent cotton.

He closed his eyes and tried to think.

He tried to move his leg. It brushed against the bars of his cage. He pulled it back as quickly as his lame muscles would respond. The reason for the thongs was self-evident now: the bars of his cage were electrically charged and the leather bands had kept his body suspended away from contact with them. Why?

Later, he heard the door slam. It shut with a dull thump of noise. It brought him back to reality though the numbness had not left his body. He stared, twisting his stiffened neck away from his arched shoulders to see what had made the noise.

A man had come between him and the iron cage that enclosed the naked body of Jerry Terry.

A tall man, muffled in a long dark cloak of some kind,

wrapped tightly about his neck. Yet if he should have hidden anything at all, he should have masked his face.

The dream-nightmare had continued.

The man's face was a grotesque mask of outraged flesh—hairless, nearly fleshless. At some time, this man had been in a great fire that had left his face a skull-like travesty of scarred tissue. His nose was merely a pair of twin holes studding the distance between the pit of a forehead and an ugly gash of mouth. His head was an encrustation of scarred, dead tissue. Only the browless eyes showed any evidence of life. And the expression they held was not . . . quite . . . sane.

"How do you like The Little Ease, Mr. Solo?" the man said, his death's-head face looming in the half-light of the cavern. "The Medieval cultures had their interesting torments, did they not? You can neither sit nor stand. Nor can you lie down. Fortunately for you, I have strapped you so that you cannot accidentally electrocute yourself. The same for the lady, of course. The electricity is, of course, a refinement we've added to the original specifications. We like to keep up to date." The eyes in the awful face seemed to glow. "You will recover the use of your voice in approximately ten minutes. If you have recovered your hearing, as I suspect you have, please nod your head."

Napoleon Solo nodded, trying hard to swallow.

"Good." The man's voice was as spectral and unreal as his appearance. It was brassy and hollow . . . like the clang of a metal door in a vault. "We must talk even though I have reduced you to these unpleasant extremes. Do not confuse the exotic nature of your torment with any wish on my part to be glamorous and occult. Nakedness is a powerful depressant, a humiliation to the feelings of the modern, so-called civilized man. It can be used as a psychological weapon, therefore." He paused. "Do you feel any physical pain as yet?"

Solo shook his head.

"Splendid. The drug always performs as desired. You would find it useful in your role as enforcement officer for U.N.C.L.E., but I'm afraid you will never see America again. At least, not unless you consent to certain articles of behavior. The same code applies to the lady. I appreciate her beauty, I assure you, and there will be much done to her before she finally ends her usefulness . . . but we were talking about the drug. It is called *anakalinine.* One tablet induces paralysis of the vocal cords for as long as two hours. You could imagine the purpose it could serve with prisoners and people one wouldn't want to have talking all about the place. You are extremely fortunate, as it is. Anyone else would have perished in that plane crash."

A dull, gnawing sensation of *pain* began to work along Solo's racked body. It began with a series of faint, hot flushes starting down from his shoulders. The cage swayed above the stone floor, adding to his sense of unreality. It must be suspended from the ceiling, Solo decided—and twisting with effort to look at Jerry Terry's cage, he saw that this was true.

"Actually, *anakalinine* also serves as a pain depressant and seems to affect the hearing as well. There are several qualities of the drug which we haven't quite explained even to ourselves as yet. No matter. Oh, forgive me. My name is Golgotha. You will appreciate the beauty of the title, considering the fact that you must be acquainted with the Christian mythos. Golgotha was the hill shaped like a skull, was it not?" The death's-head might have leered, but it was impossible to tell.

"Now, to particulars. Since a kindly fate did not allow you to die in the crash—you and the lady were thrown from the plane, since you seem to have worked the side door open even in your semi-conscious state—I have granted you a respite from death. Your fine organization cannot hurt us now. We are on the march. This time Thrush will succeed totally. Do you feel any pain now, dear Mr. Solo?"

Beads of perspiration had formed on Solo's face. From behind the tall shadow came a whimper of agony from Jerry Terry. The death's-head turned to look at her and there was a strangling noise of terror.

Golgotha laughed his metallic laugh.

"She's fainted," he said without bitterness. "Women always do at first sight of my magnificent ugliness. Rather like your Phantom Of The Opera movie, I imagine. I saw that many times as a child in Ujpest. Little did I dream that one day I would most certainly resemble your Mr. Chaney—" He broke off, as if he had betrayed himself in a moment of revelation. "No matter. Your friends are on their way back to America with Mr. Stewart Fromes' body. They will learn nothing from it. His corpse will be nothing but a skeleton by the time they reach the coast and your scientists will never trace the impossibly perfect drug which brought it all about. It leaves absolutely no trace. Think of it, Mr. Solo. A catalyst which *vanishes* once it does it work. Something your medical science has never encountered before and of course, since it will have ceased to exist, cannot encounter now. Try saying something, please."

Solo made a strangling sound in his throat. It was the barest croak of sound.

"You see? A few minutes more and you will wonder why you couldn't speak when you wanted to. So let me tell you my offer. As I say, you must die. But everything has two sides, even the matter of dying. You may die swiftly and without pain. Swallow a simple tablet, lie down, and it is ended. Or you can die by degrees, so slowly and with such monumental agony that you will scream and beg for the peace of death which I will not give you. Unless, of course, you agree to the conditions of my proposal."

Solo closed his eyes. The pain had begun to rise in waves of agony, washing down his back and thighs. He bit his lips. Golgotha would not have the satisfaction of seeing him come to heel.

"Do you hear me, Mr. Solo? Nod if you do."

Napoleon Solo nodded.

"Good. My request is simple. I want the names and locations of each and every agent known to you in the entire U.N.C.L.E. organization. This will be extremely valuable to us, as you must realize. When Thrush assumes its role as world leader, we of the Council must be certain that there are no small pockets of resistance left. It is imperative that we destroy U.N.C.L.E. You should feel flattered. We respect your organization. We regard it as our greatest threat. Do you understand? Tell me what I want to know and I will inject you with a pain-killing drug which will nullify the effects of *anakalinine*. You have only to draw up a chart containing the names and whereabouts we require."

Solo's mouth worked. He gasped for sound. The drumming fibre of Golgotha's voice was sending rivers of agony into his ears. Another minute more of this would be too much.

"W—wh—what—"

"Try, Mr. Solo. You should have voice by now."

"The—the—" It was impossible. Solo could feel the tautness of his throat.

"Breathe deeply. Shout if you must. Hear yourself."

"The—girl—same thing—"

Golgotha's eyes glittered coldly.

"Of course. I will even spare her the amorous natures of my colleagues, Mr. Solo."

"I'll do it," Napoleon Solo whispered. "But first—sleep. Must sleep—I'm out of my mind with pain—" The cage seemed to shiver with vibrations.

Golgotha stepped in closer, peering into the eyes of the man crouched before him. His voice was a menacing murmur now.

"Good. You will not be sorry. But please remember this—if you have agreed now only to say no later, you will be more sorry than I can possibly suggest. You may fool me now. But my wrath will make the gods cry out in pain."

"I promise—damn you—the needle—I can't stand this—"

Golgotha studied him intently for one second, he dug into the folds of his dark cloak and produced a flat, black medical case. Fanning it open expertly, he selected a long hypodermic needle from a velveteen bed of similar objects. Napoleon Solo's eyes followed his every movement.

The bareness of the room was still unreal. It was as if there were no door, no window, no sound from anywhere else in the wide, wide universe.

Golgotha came closer, pointing the needle at Napoleon Solo's bulging right bicep. His tongue clucked approvingly. His face, like a distended Halloween mask, was horribly near, bobbing through the metal bars of the cage.

"Your arm is like stone. I will loosen your bonds and open the door of your cage. You must flex your arm, Mr. Solo, to restore the blood circulation."

Solo nodded quickly, his eyes almost pleading now. With grim speed, Golgotha stepped before the cage and unlatched a fitted section of bars. Magically a door swung outward, showing freedom. The skull-faced man began to unwind the leather wrappings which bound Solo's right arm to a cross-work of bars. It took a mere ten seconds to loosen the cuffs. Like a dead fish, Solo's right arm fell to his side. His fingers were as senseless as if they had never been alive. Golgotha stepped back as Solo's body sagged through the narrow opening of the cage, half-in and half-out, his left arm still fastened by a thong to an iron bar.

"That's it. Work your arm up and down till the sensation returns. Otherwise the needle will never penetrate your arm, I'm afraid. Your muscles are like rock, now."

Solo nodded, gasping for air. Golgotha saw the giant tendons popping in his neck.

"—Better now—" Solo gasped. "The needle—now, please—"

Golgotha, eyes glittering, stepped forward.

And Napoleon Solo's free right arm came down in a murderous swath of released fury, meeting him full across the neck where it joined his cloaked shoulder.

A Karate blow that hammered Golgotha to the stone floor.

TERROR WALKS UNDERGROUND

NAPOLEON SOLO stared down at the crumpled, cloaked heap that formed the man who had introduced himself as Golgotha, member of the high Council of Thrush. Dimly, he fought against the agony in his body, even as his right hand worked loose the stiff, leather cuffs that bound his left arm to the cage bars. A dull haze of enormous weariness of body and spirit hung over him like a shroud. He only knew one pounding truth, one complete clarity. They had to get out—he and Jerry Terry.

Golgotha had underestimated him, as so many of the enemy had in the past. Golgotha had miscalculated the time. True, the pain would emerge when the drug *anakalinine* wore off, but Solo had triggered the error in Golgotha's eyes by acting the part. He had bargained for one chance in a million and won.

He shook his head to clear it, his body damp and aching. His eyes explored the empty dungeon. The bare walls of stone and the faint suggestion of moisture mocked him. Shaking himself, he stumbled to where Jerry Terry knelt caged as a rag doll. It took him a great deal longer to ease her carefully from her cell. When he caught her in his arms, her weight nearly bore him to the floor. Her body was cold and stiff, nearly lifeless. He slapped her swiftly across the face—hard. The sound of short, sharp smacks echoed hollowly in the room.

Her eyes opened. She saw his face and sudden joy reflected in her eyes. Then she remembered and her mouth formed another scream. He slapped her again.

"Listen—no time to talk—pull yourself together—we're okay for awhile—"

"Solo—I'm so tired—"

"Try—please—try—or we're done for—"

He left it at that, and moved back to the inert man on the floor. It took an age for him to pull the voluminous cloak away and examine the tall figure. Solo's eyes saw the withered, burned flesh of the man but his brain made no comment. His fingers found the flat medical case and thumbed it open. He tried to think. The pain was beginning to build in earnest now.

He groped for the hypodermic needle lying on the stone floor. The gods were good: it was intact. He examined the contents of the case with painful slowness. There was a tiny phial of amber fluid lying in cushioned safety in the case. He didn't stop to think; he didn't dare consider the possibilities. Grimly, he refilled the hypo and found the soft area of his arm below the bicep. He jabbed the needle home. He worked his arm up and down, wanting the pain-killer—if that was what it was—to work swiftly.

He moved slowly back to Jerry Terry. She was huddled on the stone floor, her arms closed across her naked breasts. Her entire attitude was defeated dull, lifeless. Solo smiled bitterly. Golgotha had been right about that, for all of his hideous theatricality.

Jerry never saw the needle or felt the thrust. He patted her gently on the shoulder now. Her head came up. Their eyes met in mutual sympathy.

"Terry—we're going for broke—"

"I'm with you, Solo."

"Good girl. Pull yourself together. I'll get you out of this—"

"Promises, promises—"

Her plucky talk was infectious. It was talk he could always understand. He had never had much time for people who felt sorry for themselves. And magically, almost miraculously, he could feel the agony ebbing away from his limbs. Golgotha's panacea was already working.

He went back to Golgotha and bent over him again. The Karate blow was good for at least twenty minutes. Sometimes—depending on the man's physical makeup —more. Solo raced through the cloak, turning it inside out. By the grace of those same gods, the man was a souvenir collector . . . not one to leave the spoils of war to the hirelings.

Golgotha wore a blue shirt and blue trousers under the cloak. A uniform of sorts, with a leather belt complete with assorted weapons—one of which was Solo's own very special "S" automatic pistol. A quick survey of the pockets turned up Solo's compass watch and the ball-point pen which, in addition to writing with ink, also spurted tear gas. The wallet was not in evidence, but that was meaningless anyway. With an almost intoxicating sense of elation, Solo relieved Golgotha of a compact Luger and three clips of extra ammunition. There was nothing on the man to indicate any connection with Thrush.

Solo turned to see how Jerry Terry was doing. He was pleased to find some color back in her face. And the sagging, defeated look had gone.

"Are you game for some more double plays?" he asked.

She nodded. "Anything to get out of this place."

"Good girl. We can't operate like September Morn. So the next best thing is Dream Man's clothes. I'll take the pants and shirt. You for the cloak. Unless you're squeamish. He's as foul as they come and it's twisted his mind, but we can't walk out of here like nudists. We'd be a bit conspicuous."

"Anything you say, Solo."

He nodded. "No telling when his team will show up. His body is covered with scars. So if you don't want to look, don't."

He didn't wait for her answer. Golgotha had moaned faintly. It was hardly a sound, but Solo bent swiftly to the unpleasant task of undressing the man. It took a full five minutes of struggling exertion. Golgotha was tall and heavy despite his lankiness of form.

Solo left him lying face down on the stone floor, his enflamed, withered flesh revealed to the light, grotesquely unreal in T-shirt and boxer shorts.

The clothes were a bad fit, but they would serve. Solo rolled up the cuffs and hitched the belt a notch tighter. The cloak, a heavy woolen affair with poncho type sockets for Jerry Terry's arms to thrust through, would at least keep her warm.

"Well," she sighed. "We're dressed for the ball and we look a sight but like the man said, what do we do now?"

"The door."

"Huh?"

"It's time to take a look outside. The door is thick or

else no one's been on guard duty. In any case, it's high time we found out just how bad off we are."

He motioned her to the other side of the door, which was no more than a slab of stone set tightly in the wall, with an iron handle jutting from the mass. Golgotha moaned again, and Solo cursed as he stepped quickly to him. He rapped the skull quickly with the butt end of the Luger. Golgotha subsided once more.

They waited at the door, listening. No sound issued forth. Solo frowned. He didn't like the silence or the fact that no one had shown up in all the time Golgotha had been with them. Possibly the man had issued strict orders for everyone to keep out. Twisted egos always had their shortcomings, and one of them was the "Me-Me-Me" attitude.

Solo gestured for Jerry Terry to step back. He took the iron handle and turned it. A latch clicked. Carefully, he tugged the stone backwards.

There was a sudden wash of cool air from the outside. Solo peered quickly around the rim of the door.

Semi-darkness met his eyes. He blinked. A dim glow of light, as though from a miner's lamp, filtered toward him. He stared at the ground. It was damp, muddy earth. Strange. Golgotha's boots had been dry. He signaled to Jerry Terry to follow him. She moved swiftly, the cloak wrapped about her shapely figure, her long, copper hair flying.

They were in a tunnel of some kind. A long, low passageway with timbers and beams shoring the sides and the earthern ceiling. Cool air was fanning through the tunnel from some distant, unseen opening. Solo closed the stone door, held his left hand behind him for

Jerry to take. She squeezed it warmly and they pushed on through the dimness.

The shaft narrowed suddenly, forking in two directions like the cross-bar of a T. Solo hesitated, as his eyes tried to search the darkness ahead. Grinning to himself, he moistened the forefinger of his right hand and held it up. Almost immediately, the influx of air evaporated the dampness on the right side of his finger.

"Right," he murmured. "God bless the Boy Scouts."

The clinging mud beneath their feet was firm enough to allow easy passage. Jerry had no shoes and her bare feet made slick, slapping sounds. It was unavoidable now and too late to remedy the oversight.

Solo was puzzled. What could all this lack of protection mean? No sentries or guards. No security. Was it possible that Golgotha had handled the two of them all by himself? A lone wolf caper to bargain for higher power in the Thrush Council? No, it wasn't likely. And yet there must be some explanation for all this. It was beginning to look as if they could walk right out of the spider's web into the sunlight.

Up ahead, the glow of light widened. The darkness was dissolving. The air current had increased in volume. He knew they were getting closer to the surface, without not knowing how far was Down in the first place.

Then they both heard the sound.

It came suddenly, with frightening loudness and nearness—a roaring, rhythmical throb of gigantic pistons of some kind. The beat mounted with ear-shattering violence. They flattened against the earthern walls of the passageway, trembling, waiting. Then the sound ended as abruptly as it had begun. The new silence was awesome. Solo licked his dry lips.

"What was that?" Jerry whispered.

"Turbines or pistons. I really can't say—"

"Maybe there's a plant overhead."

"Maybe. Let's keep on going and play it by ear."

They moved on again, toward the light. It had seemed closer than it was. They panted down the passageway, feeling their path in the gloom. Solo didn't dare risk using his pencil flash. They'd been too lucky as it was.

The roar of engines throbbed again. The sound had faded somewhat, meaning they had passed beneath it a few minutes back. But the pounding, humming noise was eerie and somehow terrifying. When the silence fell again, Solo realigned his grip on the automatic pistol. No telling what lay ahead now.

If Golgotha had been discovered—

Solo saw the man before the man saw him. He drew up so sharply that Jerry Terry ran into him but she had enough presence of mind not to cry out.

Solo held her back, flattening them both against the passageway. The man up ahead had his back to them. He was a silhouette framed against the daylight.

He wore a uniform of some kind—belted middle, puffy jodphurs and boots, and a peaked helmet. More importantly, a stocky, ugly looking grease gun was cradled in the crook of his arm.

Solo pushed Jerry Terry back. "Stay here," he commanded. "We can't walk past that one. He'll have to be taken."

"Be careful."

He smiled to himself at the obviousness of her concern, and moved stealthily along the wall. The man was a scant thirty yards away. Thirty yards and freedom.

But the grease gun was something to think about. It could spray them down in seconds and no real marksmanship was called for. Solo held his breath as he swiftly and soundlessly bridged the gap between them before he made his move.

And then he stepped on something that snapped in half with the loudness of a pistol shot. A dry twig. In the mud of the tunnel of all places. The irony was too cruel to be funny—and Solo did not feel like laughing. He was caught flat-footed.

The man with the grease-gun revolved as though on a swivel. His gun came up and his hoarse, guttural voice cried out challengingly. His cry echoed down the passageway.

"Vast ist?"

Napoleon Solo fired, straight from the shoulder this time, a steady burst of three, at the shadowy figure framed in the entranceway.

The tunnel reverberated with the sound of death.

THE MAN WITH THE SKULL

ALL HELL broke loose.

Even as Solo saw his three shots hit home, picking up the man in the entranceway and smashing him back, the entire passageway suddenly came alive with the ringing of bells. It was a shocking assault on the ear-drums. The air of the tunnel seemed to be alive with the high, almost screaming sound.

Fortunately, he had hurtled forward, following up the death blasts of his pistol, and Jerry Terry had fol-lowed. They reached the fallen sentinel even as they saw what was happening. A rumbling sound came from overhead, cutting through the pealing of the bells. Solo shot a look skyward. A gigantic slab of concrete was coming down, a secret door to seal the passageway to the outside world. Frantically, he seized Jerry by the wrist and pulled her through—just before the massive concrete door thudded shut between them and free-dom, sending mounds of dirt and mud flying upwards.

Behind the stone door, the bells continued their mad cacophony. A simple device. It took only the firing of a gun to set up a walled blockade in the subterranean fortress.

Jerry Terry was sobbing softly, her nerves coming un-done at last. He let her cry in peace and stared at their surroundings. They were in the open, the side of some mountainous shelf of rock. Ahead was brown country ground and a thin smattering of gnarled trees. A crow was cawing from one of the branches. Overhead, foggy sunlight washed down over them. It was so still out here, compared to the madhouse inside.

"Come on," he urged. "We still have to make a run for it."

She nodded, her eyes showing she was still game. She was a peculiar vision stumbling along in Golgotha's cape, her long, copper-colored hair catching random rays of sunlight.

They began to run in earnest, following a broken trail

of stone and sand which seemed to wind downwards to lower levels. Solo kept his eyes open, the automatic pistol ready. It was such a peculiar setup there was no way of knowing what they could run into.

The road ended, spewing them into a flat table of land which showed a vast unbroken meadow stretching almost as far as the eye could see, only to end before the towering majesty of the Bavarian Alps. Solo cursed. Damn the terrain. It was all of a piece; one place looked exactly like another.

"Solo," Jerry said softly. "Look."

He didn't see what she meant at first because of the camouflaging gnarled trees. Then his eyes cleared, making out the dark outlines of the MIG fighter. It sat, silent and ready, directly under a canopy of branches, its nose pointed toward the wide meadow before it. Only three hundred yards away.

There was no one in sight. But the bells were still sounding faintly somewhere and there was no time to lose. It was now or never for both of them.

"Jerry, listen."

"I'm way ahead of you. Let's move out."

He was glad she understood. "Okay. We'll be clay pigeons if anybody is watching. On the other hand, we're dead anyway. May I say it's been nice knowing you?"

"Forget it. We're going to get out, Napoleon, and we can take up the subject there."

He kissed her briefly, nodding half to himself, and then sprinted for the plane, knowing she would follow as best she could. He ran with his head low, his legs churning, putting forth everything he had for the run. There was no sense in looking back, no point in trying to pick out targets for the automatic. Either way, they had nothing but time on their side. Time, surprise and the fact that they were fast-moving targets.

Once, Solo had competed in the hundred yard dash at college. He had come in first, a stride ahead of the number two man, but he had never forgotten the fever of the lungs from such a run, the flying spurt of the body as it strained for the tape. Even as he had plunged across the finish line to the cheers of the stadium, he had never forgotten the almost drunken exaltation of success.

It was something like that now.

The meadow grass disappearing beneath his heels, the plane looming closer, the expectation of a burst of gunfire, the fierce straining of his muscles. He was only dimly aware of Jerry Terry's figure somewhere behind him. He could only keep his eyes to the left and right, a periphery of perhaps ninety degrees. There was nothing to alarm him from the front. The ship was unprotected. It was only the area behind them that disturbed him.

The first shot came, a singing, whining crack of sound across the flatlands. Dirt geysered somewhere near his heel. Another crack, two more.

He reached the ship and turned, just in time to catch Jerry Terry stumbling before him, falling to the earth. He stilled the alarm in his chest and picked up his targets.

Two uniformed men, rifles leveled, were stationed in the rocky recesses of the lowlands before the mountain. Too far away for his pistol to be of much use. Yet he blasted away all the same and had the extreme satisfaction of seeing them both duck back frantically.

Quickly, he helped Jerry up the wing, practically hurling her into the cockpit. It was only designed to accommodate one person but they were not about to concern themselves over such trifling matters just now. She fell in. The cloak caught on a rivet screw but she was all right as far as he could tell.

"I don't know if I can fly one of these—" she panted.

"You won't have to," he said. "I'll do it. Scrunch down and away we go."

He found the controls, emptying the pistol as he clambered in. But the men were up and running now, coming on fast as they realized how close the quarry was to getting away. Solo had a bad few seconds trying to decipher the Russian words on the instrument panel but a plane was a plane be it a Flying Jenny or MIG. The rocket starters were going to be the big question mark, never mind the basic principles of aerodynamics. Solo found the release buttons, blessing Korea, where he had acquired skimpy knowledge of the MIG Fighter Plane, from one that had come down on the banks of the Yalu River ten minutes away from Solo's Reconnaissance Patrol.

Crack!

Crack!

Two rifle shots were lost in the budding blast of the takeoff. The rockets whooshed with noise. He dug out the Luger, sighted quickly and got a shot off. One of the running soldiers suddenly dropped his rifle and rolled crazily on the turf. The other kept on coming.

From that moment on, getting off the ground was his only consideration. With Jerry Terry cramped into the narrow space between him and the floor of the ship, Solo eased back on the controls. With a powerful rush of speed, the MIG nosed forward, sending leaves flying before the tremendous backwash. The thunder of the engines drowned out all else.

The ship shot forward, thrusting like a rocket. The wheels lifted, the sun flooded Solo's face, and the wide, clear sky stretched before them.

Below, the soldier aimed a final futile shot that died on the wind.

"Jerry, see if you can work that radio. We'll contact NATO radar before they send some flyboys up to shoot us down. Not too sure about the border flyers around here. Jerry—"

It was only then that he saw the girl was bleeding.

A streak of scarlet was painting her right hand.

"Hey," he began. "What gives?"

"Oh, that smarts," she murmured drowsily, closing her eyes in pain, exhaustion and shock.

The thundering blast of the MIG drowned out Napoleon Solo's fluent curses.

Golgotha sat before a short-wave radio set, complete with amplifiers and headphones. He had found another cloak. Such expression as his face could show registered extreme hatred. In his fantastically unreal voice he spoke of his displeasure.

It was exactly one hour since he had recovered in the dungeon room to find himself shamed and disgraced. By the reckoning of the account from the guards, the man Solo and his lady confederate had escaped in the MIG, sometime in that elapsed period of sixty minutes. Even the intricate network of alarm bells had been fruitless. Obviously, this Solo was a resourceful man. There was some vindication at that. Golgotha had warned the

Council repeatedly that U.N.C.L.E. was not to be dismissed so lightly.

"I repeat, most strongly, we must continue with Plan M. I see no reason to delay. It is imperative that we move now if we are to convince the democracies that we have a weapon which will make them heed our demands. U and S should have sufficed—but they were so small scale, they served only our test purposes. Now, we must move ahead to the larger considerations. Therefore I respectfully advise that Plan M go into effect immediately."

A voice spoke up from the amplifier.

"The corpse of Stewart Fromes?"

"They will gain nothing from it," Golgoath chuckled with deep satisfaction. "A skeleton will reveal little, I see no reason to worry on that score."

"You are certain he had none of the element secured anywhere on his person?"

"None whatsoever. In dying, he had only had time to dress himself. A small curiosity there—and one our research department might well explore. The element had confused him so thoroughly and upset his mental processes, that he attired himself *in reverse.*"

"Repeat that. I do not understand."

Golgotha clarified the subject of how Stewart Fromes' corpse had been attired when claimed by Napoleon Solo.

"Excellent, Golgotha. Excellent! Council will be pleased. Another successful residue of your element. Perhaps you are right."

Golgotha's cavernous eyes gleamed.

"You will recommend Plan M, then?"

"Yes, I think I will. We are ready to make our move now, I should say."

"You make my day," Golgotha crowed. "Never fear about Napoleon Solo—I will exterminate him as soon as it is feasible. At best, he is no more than an efficient enemy agent."

The voice on the amplifier didn't care one way or the other.

"Do as you see fit. I will contact you at the same time tomorrow."

"Farewell."

"Farewell, Golgotha."

The man with the skull removed the headset from his twisted stumps of ears. His mouth parted, uttering a noise of inner ecstasy. The moment would come when all the world would know of his genius. And Thrush itself must elevate him to the Council.

Plan U had been Utangaville.

Plan S had been Spayerwood.

Plan M would be *Munich*.

Napoleon Solo eased the MIG down in a short approach, mindful of the twin patrol planes hugging his tail. As he had expected, they had been intercepted barely twenty minutes out of Orangeberg. There was no use arguing. The MIG could have easily outdistanced the two patrol planes—they were no competition in the speed department, being mere monoplanes of the Cessna design. But there were two considerations. First, they could call out the whole air force, and second, Jerry Terry was unconscious. She needed doctoring fast. Therefore when the harsh, guttural voice broke in on his radio set, which he had left open intentionally, he saw no other course but swift cooperation.

The landing strip was a long, concrete runway set down somewhere in German territory. Solo lowered his landing gear, cut his flying speed and waited grimly. Landings were far trickier than takeoffs. Coming in at better than a hundred and twenty miles an hour would be no picnic.

It wasn't.

The MIG bounced like a rubber ball, tires screaming and burning. But Solo had the satisfaction of bringing it down in one piece. After that, the rest would be gravy. Once he had explained his position to the NATO officials it ought to be fairly simple. He climbed stiffly from the cockpit, easing Jerry Terry to a standing position. He kept his eyes open, anxious to evaluate the amount of interest his strange appearance had fostered. A MIG had to be trouble in this day and age.

There was a stone Administration Building of sorts and a long, low hangar not too large in size. Possibly a remote outpost, strategically situated. France was still to the west. He checked the range of mountains showing behind him. And then there was no more time to look for outstanding landmarks. The small airfield was in an uproar.

Uniformed men were rushing from the Administration Building, rifles at high port. The patrol planes had taxied into view behind him, turning sharply to face his own plane, like matching bookends. Solo didn't wait for any further activity. He jumped to the ground, feeling the concrete jar his feet. Jerry Terry, as compactly as she was built, felt very heavy.

He heard footsteps behind him and a click of rifle

bolts driving home. And then a maddeningly familiar voice said:

"We meet again, Mr. Solo. And as you see, I am not as expendable as all that."

He froze, a sudden recognition dawning with the subtlety of a thunderclap. He turned, forcing himself to smile.

"Well, well. Heard any loud humming sounds lately?"

Standing before him, dressed in an official looking gray uniform, was Denise Fairmount. Even boots, jodphurs, visored cap and the German luger jutting from her smooth fingers could not hide the beauty of her face and figure.

"Yes, Mr. Solo. And now it will be my turn to hand out the punishment. Take him. See that the girl isn't shamming. And then bring Mr. Solo to my office. There are a few questions he must answer."

Napoleon Solo shrugged.

Thrush again. And he had flown right into their waiting arms.

"KISS ME BEFORE YOU DIE"

THE PRIVATE interview began within ten minutes of their unscheduled landing: Solo was thankful for small favors. For some reason, Denise Fairmount seemed to be in charge here and she wanted to question him privately.

"You're not looking eminently officerish, Denise. I rather like you in that uniform. Though I must say I much prefer silver lamé on lady agents."

"Please spare me your sarcasms. We may be alone, but I've only to press a buzzer and you will be extremely incapable of escaping from this place alive. Also, as you see, I have a Luger."

He remained seated in the hard-backed wooden chair. She had ushered him into this tiny cubicle in the stone building and was now esconced behind a low metal desk, idly training a dark Luger at his heart. It would be useless to try anything sudden or ill-timed. She knew it and he knew it.

She had removed the visored hat and placed it to her left on the desk. Her dark hair was wound in a severe yet attractive bun behind her neck.

"You should have told me you were a Colonel back in Paris," Solo said lightly. "We could have had all kinds of fun saluting and marching back and forth."

She frowned at him, her eyes cautious.

"Yes, I am a Colonel. I have until now killed twenty-seven men. I will kill more. I will kill *you* when the time comes. I tell you all this so that we will not waste each other's time with the sentimentalities of the Hotel Internationale. You were an assignment then, however pleasant. And you still are. But that is all you will ever mean to me, Napoleon Solo."

"If you say so, Colonel."

He had already measured distances and opportunities, and concluded with regret that nothing could be accomplished in this office. It was so small that the woman would have little to do but start blasting away. A lady with twenty-seven notches on her Luger would have no difficulty managing the twenty-eighth one.

"I am interested in what you have to say, Solo."

He smiled. "It's nice to know I have a ready audience, anyway. But what about the girl? There's nothing she can tell you."

"When she is revived, she will be brought here. One can find out many things when two prisoners are involved, don't you think?"

He shrugged. "She doesn't mean anything to me."

Denise Fairmount laughed. "Perhaps not. But I've been instructed to take the chance. The unit you escaped from has lost their opportunity. When your escape was relayed here, we waited. I must confess I never thought I'd see you again."

"You're seeing me. Now what do we do?"

She showed her teeth in a smile, but her eyes were cold.

"You are to provide a list of names, I understand."

"Is that all you want? I've got a million of them. Daniel Boone, George Washington, Dwight Eisenhower, my aunt Trudy—"

"Stop it!" she snapped, her military composure breaking. "Foolish talk will get you nowhere. Would you like to watch while the girl dies? It won't be a pleasant death, I assure you."

"I can think of several other things I'd prefer," he admitted.

There was a black telephone on the desk. Solo could see that Denise Fairmount was expectant, waiting for it to ring. He gauged the distance between himself and the desk. Too far. He would have to find another way.

"What's a nice girl like you doing in the spy business, Denise?"

Her dark eyebrows shifted in surprise.

"I believe in the future of what I am doing. The same, no doubt, as you do. That is reward enough. And when the day comes—" She paused, catching herself.

"Go on," he urged. "You were going to say something about today Europe, tomorrow the world? The song never changes, does it? Only different people sing it from time to time."

Her eyes flashed and the Luger jutted menacingly across the top of the desk.

"You are an idiot," she said quietly. "I should kill you now and claim you attempted to escape."

"Why don't you, then? I can make it look good. I'll reach across the desk and kiss you."

She bit her lip, a flush rising in her face. Her eyes narrowed and she shook her head. "No, you will not trick me. In spite of what we shared at the Internationale. There are many men yet and I am still young."

"You'll get old in this business, lady. Take my word for it."

"I only want your word on names, and places in the U.N.C.L.E. organization."

"Sorry, I'm all out of names now."

"We shall see—"

The phone rang. Deftly, she spun the receiver to her ear and listened. "Good. At once, then." She replaced the receiver. He didn't like the pleased smile on her face.

"You won't change your mind, Solo?"

"It's not my business to change my mind. I thought you knew that much about me, Denise."

She stood up, brushing her jodphurs with her left

hand and tugging the Sam Browne belt which girdled her slim waist. The Luger centered on his chest. She also returned the officer's cap to her head.

"Get up," she commanded. "And walk through that door. We shall see how much agony your lovely friend will have to endure before you begin to tell us what we want to hear. Our doctor has patched up the lady so that she will be wide awake to enjoy her coming torment."

"My, you *are* a bitch, aren't you?"

"Move," was all she said, motioning him toward the other door of the cubicle. Solo rose and sauntered toward the barrier, keeping his hands away from his body.

The door.

There was no telling what was behind the door.

It was as bad as he had expected. Worse, possibly. It was one thing to be in the soup himself, quite another to have to stand around while it was stirred with somebody he liked.

The door opened on a short corridor without illumination which led into the long, low hangar. Solo could smell the heavy odor of gasoline and grease. There was a stench like burning rubber in the air, too.

The hangar was empty of aircraft. The wide doors had been left open, hanging crookedly on their steel running bars to show the German landscape. The mountains stood poised in view beyond the tarmac.

There were just two uniformed soldiers and Jerry Terry in the building. They had formed a small semicircle in the center of the hangar. At first Solo had no notion of what they were doing until Denise Fairmount nudged him sharply with the muzzle of the Luger.

The soldiers had Jerry Terry suspended between them,

each holding one of her arms. She was made to stand straddle-legged to support her own weight without slumping. Her face was ashen and drained of life. Despite the bandaged wound of her shoulder, she was standing up and taking notice. Notice had closed her mouth in terror.

There was a metal barrier of sorts on the concrete floor. It was alive with radiant heat of some kind, glowing like a sunburst. Solo could feel the suffocating warmth as they drew nearer. There was something hopelessly cruel about the white-hot poker resting in the heart of the brazier. An electric cord ran from the handle of the thing to a wall outlet nearby. The faces of the two soldiers were dull and expressionless. Like trained seals, Solo thought. They could stick knives in a lovely girl and not raise a sweat. Or brand her with a metal-burning tool, the sort of instrument used to forge letters and numbers on steel parts.

Denise Fairmount halted him and stepped around to where she could keep him in her sights.

"Must I spell all this out for you, Solo? I could print the message across Miss Terry's face." She indicated the metal-burner and brazier.

"I get the idea. Roast lady spy if I don't open my big mouth."

Jerry Terry swallowed nervously, shaking her head, but her eyes had never left the white-hot tip of the burning poker.

"You don't like me anyway, remember, Solo? Forget it."

Denise Fairmount spun on her, viciously. "Quiet, you fool! He can save you a great deal of pain."

As Denise Fairmount glared at the girl, Solo moved

one step toward her. It was as far as he dared go with
the guards watching, but it would have to be far enough.
Denise was still well beyond arm's length, but—

Solo cleared his throat. "All right then, Denise. Unac-
customed as I am to public squealing . . ."

She turned back toward him, surprised that he was
giving in so easily. It put her off her guard just enough—

Solo's right leg shot upward and his body arched
backwards in a perfectly executed *Le Savate* kick. The
tip of his shoe caught the Luger directly under the barrel, sending it high into the air above their heads. It
flipped twice neatly and he caught it before it hit the
floor. He quickly turned it to the proper position, his
finger on the trigger.

Denise Fairmount fell back with a shriek and the two
men holding Jerry Terry released her and went for their
guns. Unfortunately for them, their weapons were slung
behind their shoulders in the required form for soldiers
bearing rifles.

Yet they were foolhardy and wouldn't stop. Released
from their grip, Jerry Terry fell hard to the floor. Denise
Fairmount, in her anxiety to regain control of the situation, went wildly for the white-hot poker in the brazier.

There was no time to shout orders or commands to
halt the carnage. The soldiers were bringing their rifles
to bear and Denise Fairmount was already brandishing
the glowing poker.

Solo's first shot caught one soldier high in the chest
and spun him around. His second found a nesting place
directly in the forehead of the other man. Both of them
were dead before they hit the stone floor of the hangar.

And then there was Denise Fairmount.

If she had stopped—if she had for a moment considered she was going up against a marksman at close quarters—he might have stayed his hand. He didn't want to shoot the woman; she could be valuable later on. But Denise Fairmount had lost all power to think coherently or to evaluate consequences. All of her headlong charge, with the poker held like a flaming rapier, was spearheaded for the body of Napoleon Solo. Unluckily for her, he didn't have the time for a fancy or well-chosen shot. The time had arrived at that split-second when all lives are changed by the next bullet.

Solo triggered the Luger once more. A single, telling shot.

He stood and watched as Denise Fairmount's face came apart with surprise and pain, as if she had never believed he would actually shoot her. The poker described a smoking eddy as it clanged to the stone, shooting off sparks. Denise Fairmount crumpled, her hands holding her Sam Browne belt as if that alone could hold her up and keep her from dying.

Wordlessly, Solo stepped over her body and lifted Jerry Terry to her feet. He kept an eye on the hangar entrance. Once again, the race would be to the swift.

Despite the obvious pain and confusion she was undergoing, Jerry couldn't take her eyes off Denise Fairmount's prone figure, curled up in death.

"Solo—you killed her—"

"You can lecture me later," he said impatiently. "Right now, I'm for that MIG and getting out of here, and nothing else."

Her eyes were dazed.

"Come on—we have to move quickly. Can you walk?"

She nodded dumbly, allowing him to half-push, half-drag her to the tarmac. Solo flung a sweeping search over the field. The MIG was where he had parked it, even facing toward takeoff. There was no sign of the two patrol planes. It seemed as if there were no one else on the field. Everybody had been accounted for.

"You wide awake now, Terry?" he barked.

"Yes. Yes!"

"All right, then. Come on. And don't look back. Just remember—it was Denise or us."

Jerry Terry said nothing further. She lowered her head and staggered for the MIG. Solo was just behind her, imploring the silent gods to stay with them for just five minutes more until he got the damn MIG airborne once again.

But even as he made the unspoken plea, he could see a heavy motor lorry turn in from the roadway about five hundred yards down the field.

Grimly, he hurried Jerry Terry ahead of him, not bothering to mention the minor detail that their flight was not unobserved.

When the hounds were on the scent, it was downright amazing how they showed up at the most inopportune moments.

What was even worse, the pain had come back. Sharp, excruciating agony coursed through his body.

Partridge of the Paris Overseas Press Club was in the bar, finding new joy in the way Stanley mixed martinis, when he was summoned to the telephone. Shrugging heroically, he lifted his bulk from the leather stool and had a houseboy plug in a phone for him.

"Partridge here," he said tiredly.

"Who gives the given signal?" a crisp voice asked.

He became alert immediately. "You do."

"Who tells the untold millions?"

"I do."

He knew it was Napoleon Solo's voice at the other end, but one had to play the code out.

"Who had a second knife?"

"The same chap who had the first one."

"Billy," Solo said. "I need your help, and pronto."

"Fire away, old sport."

"Fire one—I'm sitting at Landry's airstrip. I owe him thousands of dollars for wrecking his plane. He won't take a MIG in trade and the French Air Force is pretty mad at me for flying one in. Fire two—I've got a very sick girl friend on my hands. She could die if she doesn't see a doctor soon. Fire three—the world is in sad shape. You'd better tell my uncle all about it. No doubt he's dying to hear from me."

"I see. Landry's. Good show, old sport. Be there in two hours. I'll call your uncle, of course. Think you can hold out until then?"

"I'll try, Billy. And thanks."

"Ever the faith endures," Partridge chuckled. "Anything else?"

"No, that ought to cover the preliminaries. The girl is my first concern right now."

"Off I go."

William Partridge hung up, drummed the phone for three taut seconds of preparation, downed his martini zestfully and left the bar like a shot.

Stanley, the bartender, had never seen him move so fast.

Illya Nickovetch Kuryakin was unhappy.

In his tiny West Side apartment in Manhattan, New

York, he paced the rooms, looking for something to do. Working overtime at Headquarters had not improved his restlessness. There was just so much they had been able to discover about Stewart Fromes' corpse. And that very, very special piece of dynamite his dead toes had revealed—the tiny capsule. If it was what the lab boys expected, then things indeed would get very bad around the world.

Kuryakin tried not to think about Napoleon Solo. Awkward business liking a fellow agent. When the going got rough, as it usually did, it was a terrible thing not to be on hand to assist with the difficulty. Kuryakin was levelheaded enough to despise the Russian side of his nature which tended toward gloomy prophecy. Still, an agent of Napoleon's capabilities should be able to take care of himself—

Memory of Stewart Fromes and his capabilities made Kuryakin's brow cloud over again. Damn this infernal business of waiting, waiting, waiting. One had to be doing something at all times. It was a must.

SEND HIM TO THE CEMETARY

LONDON FOG settled like a blanket over the city. The "ruddy pea-soups" of legend and fact had closed lovingly over buildings, cobbled steets and historic landmarks. The Cumberland Hotel sat squarely in the center of the heaviest concentration of the vapors. The fog did not swirl or dance or filter. It hung curtain-like over London town.

Waverly, ensconced behind a glass-topped desk in a suite of rooms on the fourth floor, was holding court. He was dressed once more in his familiar tweeds, yet there was something jaunty about his manner. The red carnation adorning his lapel lent a touch of joviality seldom seen by his colleagues, to his appearance.

Seated at various points of the modernistically furnished room were Napoleon Solo, Jerry Terry and Illya Kuryakin. Solo wore a dark suit of conservative cut and a sober powder blue tie. His face was as unlined and freshly handsome as ever. Jerry Terry, her long copper hair neatly bound with a red headband, looked beautiful and invulnerable in a beige woolen sheath dress. The contrasting white sling in which her right arm was cradled somehow seemed an afterthought rather than a necessity.

Kuryakin's attire was less unkempt than usual. He had managed to appear in a pressed, clean suit of indeterminate gray. The atmosphere was cordial and friendly. Smoke from Solo's cigarette filled the air.

"So Partridge got you out, Solo," Waverly concluded.

"Partridge got *us* out," Solo amended, winding his account of the adventure into a neat summarization of the facts. Waverly had evinced keen interest when Golgotha had entered the narration. Even Kuryakin had never seen Waverly so drawn out before.

"Golgotha. We've been waiting for his hand in this. High time, too. Thrush had to enlist a man of his stripe sooner or later."

"He's a new one on me, Sir," Solo remarked, smiling at Jerry Terry. Memory of that flight in the MIG made him wince—wrestling with unfamiliar controls and fighting to stanch the flow of blood from her shoulder with his free hand to keep her from bleeding to death. It was all over—for the time being. They could breathe free for a bit. "I've never heard of Golgotha."

"Kuryakin," Waverly murmured.

The young Russian smiled at Solo and the girl.

"Napoleon, Golgotha is Fromes' opposite number. An absolutely brilliant chemist. Security has had him on file for years, at least up until there was a fire-explosion in his laboratory in Budapest in '54. He's been out of sight since then. Everyone assumed he was alive but had somehow been disfigured in the blast. We've been waiting for him to show up with Thrush. He's exactly the sort of man they would find use for—brilliant, embittered, and hungry for some sort of fame in his own field."

"You think he's come up with some super-drug that scored so heavily in Utangaville and Spayerwood?"

"It's a safe guess at this writing, Napoleon. The man's a wizard and our lab results check out to something frightening. In fact, if we don't find the stockpile of this unknown element, the world is in for a jarring time."

Solo frowned at Waverly. "Fromes' pellet?"

"Yes, Solo," his chief said heavily. "Our worst fears are realized now. Thrush has found a blood catalyst which causes a man to literally lose his mind and all sense of mental coordination. Lord knows what a sight those two towns must have been with the entire populace running amuck. And they've been improving their methods since then—decomposition of the body is now speeded up to less than twenty-four hours of full cyclic effect. Fromes is no more than a skeleton now."

Solo restrained a visible shudder. "What was in the pellet?"

Kuryakin laughed harshly.

"What good would the chemical composition do you, Napoleon? It's enough to say that it is a never-before-known agent. The lab is trying to break it down now. We only know what it can do. After Fromes' odd case, I tried it on guinea pigs and white mice. They lasted only three hours. If Thrush has it, we're in for it, as I said."

"Stockpile, you said," Solo mused.

"Yes," Waverly agreed. "It's their pattern. Build up enough of a supply to cover the universe. I would say so."

"That makes a lot of sense to me," Jerry Terry said. "There'd be no end of places to hide something that small. So innocuous looking too."

Waverly pyramided his lean fingers, his eyes sweeping over the three of them. He looked almost kindly for a change. They would never know how much he appreciated all three of them, at that precise moment. It was a comfort to talk with one's own kind. The experience of the jet bomber was still too fresh in Waverly's mind.

"That cemetery, Mr. Waverly," Solo suggested. "They were awfully determined about our not taking a look."

"True enough, Solo. But that cemetery checks out. Orangeberg. Built in 1922. Spared by the Allies in World War Two. If it were a blind of some kind, we'd have to have proofs. You don't go poking about cemeteries,

Solo. It just isn't done. The Queen Mother herself couldn't order such a thing."

"Queen?" There was a startled expression on Napoleon Solo's face. Waverly leaned forward, catching the odd look. He half-smiled.

"I was only being amusing, Solo. Or did you think of something—?"

"I'm not sure."

"Napoleon, what is it?" Kuryakin prodded, knowing the makeup of the man who was his fellow agent. Jerry Terry sat enthralled. The rapport between the three men was suddenly electrifying.

Mr. Waverly said gently, "You've thought of something."

"Yes, yes, wait. The word Queen did it. Queen, Queen, Queen. By Judas, that's got to be it!" Solo sprang to his feet. "Mysteries. Stew was a mystery fan. Read them by the car-load, and now I remember—his favorite was Ellery Queen!"

"Go on, Solo, go on."

The hotel suite was silent save for Solo's energetic pacing back and forth. "Wait—I haven't got it all yet. But hear me out. It helps the wheels to turn. What did we have? Stew's body with the clothes on *backwards*, right? They let him stay that way for us to find, right? So it had to be okay with them; otherwise they would have guessed he was trying to leave some kind of message after death. By God, it all falls neatly into place. They let him stay with his clothes reversed because they thought it was one of the aftereffects of their damned mind-killing drug. Yes, yes. That's got to be it or they would have switched his clothing back to normal as sure as God made rotten little agents. Don't you see?

Stewart must have been naked, maybe in the tub or something when the effects of the stuff hit him. They had to know that. And he dressed backwards and all the time they thought he wasn't coordinating—yet actually he was thinking more clearly than any man I've ever known!"

His enthusiasm and logic were contagious. His three listeners dared not interrupt lest they break the chain of his magic.

"Now, Stew knew that I knew he was a fanatical mystery fan. Above all an Ellery Queen fan. So he did the one thing to point the finger at what he had discovered. He had found the drug, stuck a pellet between his toes, but in case that was discovered, he had told us as surely as if he had written it in black letters a foot high exactly where to look. It was a long shot, a long, long shot but I feel sure it's paid off."

Waverly coughed. Napoleon Solo smiled.

"I'll keep you waiting no longer. In case you don't know, the most famous Ellery Queen mystery of them all begins with the corpse of a man found—on which all the clothing has been *reversed*. The killer did this to conceal the fact that the man had been a *priest*. Therefore the absence of the tie was not immediately apparent as it normally would have been—"

"Solo," Waverly demurred. "Priest, tie—I fail to see —"

"Let me finish. As I say, that book is Ellery Queen's most famous. Been reprinted a thousand times and people all over the world who go in for mysteries remember it. That's the important point that Stew didn't want me to miss. The *title* of that very famous book."

Jerry Terry suddenly said in a very clear voice, "Well, I'll be damned. *The Chinese Orange Mystery.*"

"Exactly. *The Chinese Orange Mystery.* Pointing to one stockpile that has to be destroyed at all costs."

There was a new silence in the room.

"Orange," Kuryakin said, almost ruefully. "What a gamble."

"*Orangeberg Cemetery,*" Waverly said with grim finality.

Oberteisendorf.

Darkness in the village. A few scattered lights. The livestock lowing in the sheds. A rural solitude dominated the hamlet at five o'clock in the morning. The sky was moody black, pierced only by an occasional star.

There was a light gleaming in Herr Burgomeister's house—a lone bulb shining steadily through the drab, linen curtains. Herr Muller was busy with a visitor: the awesome, terrifying man he knew only as *Herr.*

"*Bitte,* what you want of me now?"

"A friend of mine has passed away," Golgotha said. "He must be buried immediately."

Herr Muller's face in the harsh light of the bulb, reflected fear.

"*Ach.* Another?"

"Yes. The poor fellow died of a tumor. Brain tumor. There was no chance. It is better this way."

"*Ja, ja.*" Herr Muller sipped his glass of Rhine wine. He did not like these conferences with this strange, cloaked man. The money was fine, one hundred thousand of the new marks, but *Gott in Himmel!*—was it worth it to have to talk with this man from hell each time?

133

"The coffin will be at your friend's mortuary in the morning. You will see to it that all the arrangements are satisfactory. You must arrive at Orangeberg Cemetery no later than twelve o'clock noon. It has been agreed on that way."

"*Ja,* I do. Same as ever."

Golgotha chuckled dryly.

"You are sweating, Herr Muller. Are you warm?"

"*Ein bischen,*" muttered the Burgomeister. "A little. I feel—tired. Makes me sweat."

"Certainly."

"You must not misunderstand, *mein Herr,*" the scrawny mayor cried. "My devotion is—strong."

"It had best remain so."

The unspoken threat lingered in the closeness of the room.

"I do the job."

"You must. We have other coffins. Many, many coffins. Sometimes we actually do use them as they were intended to be used. Remember that, Herr Muller."

The Burgomeister paled. "*Ja,* I remember."

Golgotha stood up, a towering, dark shadow which cast a ghostly silhouette across the floor. He seemed all of seven feet high and as palpable as a nightmare.

"Oberteisendorf will become famous, Herr Muller. People will point to it one day and say 'There. There is the place and there is where it happened.' Greatness will come to Oberteisendorf, Herr Muller. And fame. And exalted memory. Remember that."

"I will remember," Herr Muller whispered, wishing his frightening visitor would go as silently as he always came. The man completely destroyed whatever soul he had left.

"Good. Twelve o'clock then. One coffin. Orangeberg. *Gute Nacht,* Herr Muller."

"*Gute Nacht, mein Herr.*"

With his cloak wrapped about him like a shroud Golgotha left. Herr Muller crossed himself again, as he always did, and then reached once more for the bottle of Rhine wine.

The ghastly business would begin all over again on the morrow and there was not a thing he could do to stop it.

Verdammt! What in God's name were they burying in that lovely cemetery just beyond the rimrock?

Herr Muller did not know. He was only certain of one thing. The coffins he had delivered for the *Herr* had never contained dead bodies. He did not care what the Death Certificate claimed nor how many headstones they put up with all the lying inscriptions.

Orangeberg was not a place where dead men slept.

A NICE LITTLE PLACE TO BOMB

THE PLAN WAS daring. It had to be. Events had worked to that point where no other plan of action was feasible. Waverly had consulted with whomever he had to consult and the answer had come down from on high: *Find out about Orangeberg. When you are certain, blast it off the face of the earth. We'll take the consequences, whatever they may be.*

So it was that on a foggy night later that week, a United States Air Force C-47 roared through the heavens over Europe, bound for Oberteisendorf.

Napoleon Solo sat in the passenger compartment. He was no longer sartorially elegant or well-groomed. Indeed, he was completely outfitted for a drop behind enemy lines. His flying suit was complete: helmet, goggles, fur-lined parka. His most vital possession, however, was X-757, the specially devised U.N.C.L.E. fire-explosive which produced so much heat that it could fuse an area to a depth of ten feet. Judiciously placed at Orangeberg, X-757 would reduce the cemetery to a pit of molten lava in which rock, earth, wood coffins and those hellish little capsules and their contents would lose their identities as separate substances.

Solo's entire wardrobe was built for combat operation; map, pistol and complete detonation kit. This included five pounds of nitro jelly spread harmlessly about his person. It was only when the mass was put together like butter for a cake and frosted with blasting caps that it would take on a different, far more deadly character.

Seated across the aisle from him, beside a very worried looking Jerry Terry, was Illya Kuryakin, attired in exactly the same costume. The Russian's face wore a blissful smile. Inactivity dulled him. This investigation of a cemetery in Orangeberg was more to his liking. He patted the entrenching tools fastened to his pack. Jerry Terry was busy making adjustments on a two-way radio before her. Each man had a walkie-talkie hand set which could make instant contact if they remained within a five mile radius of the plane.

"Ten minutes," the intercom from the forward cabin crackled.

Jerry flung a worried look at Napoleon Solo. He smiled at her, trying to make her feel better. He knew he was wasting his time. She was too intelligent not to know how ridiculously short the odds were. It all boiled down to suicide, even on U.N.C.L.E.'s humanitarian terms.

Waverly had remained in London long enough to prepare the details of the plan. "Remember," he had cautioned in his usual fatherly way, "You paradrop in as close as possible to your target, dig up *one* coffin. If it contains anything other than a corpse, radio the plane to make a fast pick-up and get out of there. You know what you have to do. Failing that, the bomber will carry a pay load. That could help."

Yes, it would be easy, Solo reflected. Like dropping in to tea with the Grand Duchess.

"Radio's working fine," Jerry Terry said flatly. The roar of the bomber engines was like far-off thunder.

"Good," Kuryakin said. "Communications mean a lot this trip."

"Kuryakin," she whispered suddenly. "Make yourself scarce, will you?"

He grinned, not offended. "I'll see if there's any coffee left in the commissary." He shouldered down the aisle, going forward, his pack and parachute making him seem pounds heavier.

Jerry Terry slid into the seat alongside Solo. He turned from contemplation of the dark sky beyond the wings.

"Stinker," she hissed.

"Who, me?" he said banteringly.

"Keep it up. Smile. Big hero. You could get killed on this stunt, you know that? Two to one old Skull Face is sitting down there just waiting for you to come back. You're so irresistible in your own unforgettable way."

"Am I?" he said, keeping a smile from creeping across his face.

"Oh, Napoleon." She crumpled against him, all the anger gone out of her. "Why do you have to be so irresistible? I was doing fine until you showed up, you know that? Men don't mean that much to me."

"And they do now?" he asked softly, brushing her forehead with his lips.

"Yes, no. Oh, you know what I mean."

"Jerry, listen to me."

"Tell me to be brave and I'll spit right in your eye."

"No," he agreed. "I wasn't going to say that."

She pushed away from him, searching his eyes. "No, you wouldn't. What *were* you going to say, Napoleon?"

He stared at her soberly.

"I owe this one to Stewart Fromes and a lot of other people. You understand?"

"Yes—I think I do."

"Plus which I have no intention of dying. Believe it. I like life, cigarettes and coffee. And girls."

She recognized what he was trying to say despite the mockery of his curved smile.

"You're still a stinker, Solo."

"Of course I am."

The intercom came alive again. *"Five minutes."*

They kissed. A quick warm kiss. Jerry Terry sighed and brushed a bright strand of hair from her face.

And then Kuryakin had come back, almost apologetically, checking his equipment and gear one final time.

"I am sorry," he said, "but it is just about that time."

"One minute to zero," the intercom said.

They stood in line beside the bail-out door, their drop lines secured to the long bar parallel to the cabin. The voice on the intercom began a countdown. Solo did not look back at the girl. He stared into the darkness yawning beyond the fringe of the air door.

Kuryakin was right behind him, the dour face happy. He was idly humming something that sounded vaguely Russian. A gloomy, low refrain.

The slipstream made Solo's flying suit billow. He concentrated on the voice of the inter-com:

". . . nine, eight, seven, six . . ."

Six seconds to eternity. *And the solution of Stewart Fromes' problem.*

And then five. *Had he really been right or was it all a game?*

And then four. Three. *Three to success or death.*

". . . two . . . one!"

He stepped through the air door and was caught by the wind, his line releasing him. Darkness sprang up to meet him. The engine's roar moved on. And he was falling, falling. . . .

The dark world over Orangeberg waited to meet his hurtling body.

Solo came down with a lurch on a rising hillock of ground. Luckily, he had missed the trees. His body rolled, the shrouds of his chute picking up the worst of a brisk wind which billowed the silken folds back to umbrella shape. He scrambled erect, fighting the breeze, pulling the shroud lines to him, shortening the bursting strength of the wind. Soon he had collapsed the chute and unbuckled the harness, standing on the thing before it could sail away into the darkness of the night.

He searched the sky for Kuryakin, happy to see the white mushroom of his chute making contact with the ground less than three hundred yards away. Elatedly, he balled up his pack and hurried toward his fellow agent. You could never be sure about a drop. The unexpected was always likely to happen when you least expected it.

Kuryakin had mastered his own difficulties by the time he reached him. They shook hands warmly, glad to be alive, and set about burying their silken passports to Germany.

From on high came the muffled boom of the bomber as it flashed on for a fifteen minute run toward the Russian border. On its return flight, another fifteen minutes, it would attempt to make contact with them. That gave Solo and Kuryakin exactly thirty minutes to find Orangeberg, dig up one grave, and reach a decision. One half hour to discover if they were right or wrong about the cemetery sleeping quietly in the lowlands beyond Oberteisendorf.

Kuryakin tamped the earth down on the remainder of his parachute. He grunted in satisfaction and replaced the entrenching tool on the hook fastened to his pack. The wind billowed his flying suit as he turned to Solo.

"It's your expedition, Napoleon."

"All expenses paid. I make the cemetery out due north of us according to the compass. Maybe a thousand yards. Not too bad a drop, considering."

"Recognize anything yet?"

"Hard to tell. Landmarks at night are always a fooler.

But there's a reasonable familiarity about the neighborhood. Shall we go?"

"Let's," grinned Kuryakin, his teeth flashing in the darkness. "I haven't dug a grave in years."

They worked toward the direction Solo's wrist compass indicated, finding the going amazingly even. The land was low, flat and undisturbed by foliage of any kind. Had it been a moonlit night, it would have been a cakewalk. Yet the extreme darkness was a blessing in disguise. They were, after all, in enemy territory, Golgotha's back yard, and while the possibility of land mines, booby traps and electronic alarm systems was not to be discounted there was no time to worry about incalculables.

They pushed on, finding the ground easy to traverse, watching the shadowy distance unfold before them, identifying each indistinguishable clump of earth and darkness as a potential enemy until they reached it. Solo had his automatic pistol at the ready. A night hawk cawed once and they both waited for the tell-tale sound of men moving that might follow. None came. They moved on.

The earth narrowed and the high walls of a gorge rose about them, only to level off into more flatland. Solo spotted a familiar rise in the terrain and his hopes rose with it. Something about the topography was eminently right, now. Yes, yes—there it was. The earth stopped and suddenly a long, knee-high bunker of concrete was before them. Here and there, a gleaming tombstone winked white in the darkness, its stone angles catching random stabs of reflected light.

"Napoleon—" Kuryakin whispered.

"Yes. Orangeberg. Let's find a dead one."

"Right. No sense in pushing our luck. We'll take the first one we come across. I want to stay as close to the wall as possible."

"Check."

They slipped over the wall, careful to keep their many items of equipment from making undue noises. Their boots made contact with soft dry ground. The even, terraced nature of the earth was not lost on them. A row of headstones, barely twenty-five yards away, poked eerily into view.

The utter desolation of Orangeberg was now readily apparent. An almost palpable silence hung over the cemetery. An aura of everlasting stillness. Solo had seen Orangeberg from the air and understood the vast size of the place. Yet down here, the sensation was one of telescoping in size, as if in microcosm—it was only another burying place like a million other nameless ones all over the world. It was an odd sensation. The miles had shriveled down to the twenty five yards that was as far as his eyes could make out in the darkness. Were it not for the silvery shafts of the headstones just before them, they might have stood in any gloomy vacant lot.

There seemed to be no caretaker's house or night watchman to contend with. Yet it was impossible to tell. They would have to operate as though discovery were imminent and they might have to shoot their way out any second.

Solo reached the headstone that was closest, a square slab of marble, barely knee-high. It was placed directly between two oblong arches of granite.

"Here," he whispered, unfastening his shovel from the pack on his back. "This one will do. The smaller the better."

Kuryakin nodded and moved abreast of him.

Solo bent down, cupping his pencil flash and beaming it directly on the slab. The engraved Old English lettering on the stone was bold and final in its epitaph:

WILHELM VANMEYER

1919—-1959

Requiescat En Pace

Solo and Kuryakin exchanged dour glances.

"Latin and German don't exactly go together," Kuryakin muttered.

"No," Solo agreed. "But these are a collection of books we can't afford to judge by their covers. Dig."

Grimly, they set to, easing their spades into the ground. It was tougher going than they might have expected. Here, on the outer perimeter of the cemetery, the earth was considerably harder. Ruefully, Solo now remembered a peculiarity of burying grounds: the borders of most of them tended to be the less ideal ground for interment. Which was why most vaults and crypts turned up at the entranceways and gateways of cemeteries. Not because the richest corpses wanted to be showed up front. Still, it should be only a matter of moments—if there were no interruptions.

They dug quickly, making a dark mound of uncovered earth to one side of the slab. It didn't take too long. Solo's spade thucked hollowly on a box of some kind. The sound spurred them on. Soon they had cleared a sufficient amount of space about the top of a simple pine coffin.

The box had not been six feet down. Three was much nearer the mark.

"If there's a skeleton in there, I promise to defect to the Russians," said Kuryakin.

"Fair enough. And I'll do the Watusi in Macy's window on Christmas Day. Ready?"

"Ready."

The lid came off, pried loose by their straining fingertips, after Solo had raced a claw hammer about the edges to speed things along. There was a creak of wood and suddenly the lid was free, pulling back in Kuryakin's startled hands. Overhead, the wind sighed across the graveyard, as Solo thumbed his pencil flash on once again and played its beam over the contents of the coffin.

A twinkling galaxy of clustered stars lay revealed in the dime-sized circle of light.

Round silver balls, identical with the one placed between the toes of Stewart Fromes' corpse, lay boxed by the thousands in the coffin before their eyes. The coffin was filled almost to lid level with them. They were like some mammoth collection of ball-bearings saved by a fanatic collector of the things. But Solo knew they were nothing so harmless as all that.

"Bingo," said Solo, "and end of the search."

"Napoleon," Kuryakin said in an odd, tight voice. "Don't move too fast. We're being infiltrated upon and though I hate to say so—we're surrounded."

Solo cursed and turned the pocket flash off, rolling to the ground. Yet even as he did so, the dark cemetery lit up with the brightness of full daylight as powerful searchlights trained their traveling beams on the headstones that marked the bogus resting place of Wilhelm Vanmeyer.

"*You will stand as you are and do nothing*," the funereal

voice of the man called Golgotha yelled hollowly across the open ground, *"or you will most certainly die before we have a chance to talk again."*

GOLGOTHA AGAIN

THE SEARCHLIGHTS were blinding. Caught in the merciless exposure, Solo and Kuryakin were like two shafts sticking in a mammoth circular dartboard. Beyond the dazzling glow of the beams, once their eyes had become adjusted to the light, they could barely make out the tall shadows of the men behind the glare.

Solo raised his arms, blinking his eyes to clear them, saying out of the side of his mouth to Kuryakin:

"Let me do the talking."

Kuryakin, grotesquely unreal in his flying suit, loaded down with equipment, the walkie-talkie hung from his throat like a lantern, nodded slightly.

"Golgotha!" Solo called. "Can you hear me? It is important that you do!"

There was a murmuring rumble of voices from the direction of the glare. Then came a fierce German guttural for *"Silence!"* and the metallic, almost lazy voice of Golgotha floated on the night air.

"Yes, Mr. Solo, I hear you. What do you propose to say?"

Solo blinked in the lights.

"Tell your army not to fire at us. We are wired with explosives. Enough to blow this cemetery and all of us to Berlin and back. Let me make that very clear—shoot us and you destroy yourself! Shall I repeat the message?"

A hard, mocking laugh rode the wind.

"Really, my dear Solo. Such melodramatics. You would die so readily for U.N.C.L.E.?"

Napoleon Solo shrugged and stared back into the lights. A tight smile held his mouth rigid.

"Suit yourself. Take the long shot—tell them to shoot. We knew the risk we took coming in here. But remember—when we die, so dies your glorious plan for the element which you so cleverly stockpiled in this cemetery. Throw away your years of planning. It will be worth it."

Several of the bright, dazzling beams cut off with the suddenness of a thrown switch. The newer darkness was as pleasant and gratifying as fresh air after a long submersion in the water. Dimly, Solo could now make out the tall figure of Golgotha behind the remaining lights, his cloaked figure rising from the graveyard like some ghostly specter of the imagination. More importantly, there were four more uniformed figures flanking him at intervals of five yards, sub-machine guns at the ready.

Kuryakin rumbled in his throat like a trapped lion. Solo hoped his impetuous partner would sit on his impatience to move into action.

"Solo," Golgotha said. "I believe you. Now, may I ask what sort of bargain you ask me to make for your lives? You are not suggesting I turn you loose?"

Napoleon Solo laughed.

"You heard the bomber upstairs a while ago? It dropped us off. If they don't hear from us in ten minutes, they will know that we were captured or killed and they will go ahead with the target for tonight. I leave you to guess what that is."

There was a harsh intake of air. He saw the figure of Golgotha raise its skeletal arms and bring them down together in crackling anger. He had pegged the man correctly. To see the bubble burst after so many years of careful building must have been a crushing blow. Solo was banking on Golgotha's mammoth ego to assist their escape from this deep, deep hole.

"Tell me, Solo. What excuse would the U.S. have for bombing a peaceful German cemetery in the middle of nowhere?"

Solo threw his head back and laughed.

"Be yourself, Golgotha. We have a sample pellet of the contents of your coffin stockpile. No matter what wreckage the bomber makes here, investigators will find enough of the pellets to justify the obliteration of a menace to world peace. Then the evidence of Utangaville and Spayerwood will speak out loud and clear. Well, hurry up—time is very literally on the wing."

Kuryakin, without a signal from Solo, unhooked his walkie-talkie and reached for the antennae.

"Wait!" the voice of Golgotha screamed. But Solo repressed a smile of triumph. The man's voice was hesitant now. Was the bluff working?

There was nothing to be done yet, not with that ring of sub-machine guns trained on them. It all depended on the weird brain of the devil who commanded them.

"Solo!"

"I'm listening."

"Call the plane. Tell them you were wrong. There is nothing here. Tell them to come down and pick you up."

"Then what?"

"We will bargain."

"What kind of bargain? I give you the United States and you give me Russia?"

"Don't play the fool, Solo. Whatever your lofty ideals are, I'm sure you're still interested in living."

Solo hesitated, making his hesitation visible and obvious. He bit his lip, flinging a look at Kuryakin. The Russian shrugged. Solo turned back to face Golgotha and the lights and the threat of the guns. Time was all he and Kuryakin needed, really.

"All right," he said. "I'll call. But no tricks, Golgotha. That plane is loaded with army men who won't take anything lying down, so if you have any notions about capturing the whole lot of them, forget it."

He unharnessed his own walkie-talkie and set it on the ground before him. But Golgotha had stepped forward, one hand raised in authority. To all ears now, came the powerful throb of the bomber. The roar of its jet engines returning from the Russian border blasted toward the cemetery.

"Just a moment," Golgotha said icily. "I wish to hear whatever you have to say to them."

"Come ahead," Solo said. "It's your party." As he waved his arm, the gesture allowed the concealed trench knife strapped upside-down on his forearm to slide handle-first into the palm of his hand.

"Yes," Golgotha said. "I shall come. But do not, I warn you, commit the mistake of treachery. Death is not such a fear to me that I will not save myself for the last laugh. You will blow up, you say. But I do not think you would have risked the parachute jump thus armed. Yet I cannot afford to guess, so I parry with you. All I lose for the moment is time, which is not so precious to me as it is to you. I find it hard to believe your bomber would destroy the field with men such as yourself in doubt, but we shall see. So make your call—but remember, you are covered by four sub-machine guns."

He came forward across the ground, skirting a tombstone, his ghastly figure unreal in the lights. Kuryakin, who was seeing him for the first time, stifled an oath. Even Solo had to admit that Golgotha—hard to take under ordinary conditions—was a leftover from a very bad nightmare when seen here in a searchlight-flooded cemetery.

Golgotha halted about ten feet away from them. He pointed a bony forefinger.

"Call the bomber," he said hollowly.

Solo switched on the walkie-talkie. It hummed with static, until he found the circuit that Jerry Terry was tuned in on. Carefully, while his brain raced, his right hand balanced the handle of the trench knife.

Kuryakin had abandoned his set. He was staring at the four shadows behind the glare of the lights. Solo knew Kuryakin was busy too, but he wished fervently that he knew exactly in what way.

"Baker, this is Sugar," Solo said distinctly into the mouthpiece. "Baker this is Sugar. Over."

The walkie-talkie hummed with static. Solo strained for the answer that he knew would not come. He was keeping his forefinger on the receiving lever, using only the sending half of the set. The bomber and Jerry Terry would hear his voice but the answer would never sound from the set. He hoped hard that neither Golgotha nor any of his minions had had any previous experience with the Army Walkie Talkie, Ml.

"Baker, this is Sugar," he repeated, letting desperation enter his voice. "Come in, please." He was sure Kuryakin had tumbled to what he was doing. But he turned to him and winked: "Something's wrong. I can't reach the plane."

"Let me try my set," Kuryakin agreed readily.

Golgotha muttered hollowly in his throat.

"You seek to trick me?" He stared up at the heavens, unable to see the bomber or its riding lights though the roar of the plane filled the heavens. Solo turned, his arms outstretched.

"Don't be stupid," he gritted. "They'll blow us up if they don't hear from us soon. What time is it, Kuryakin?"

"We have three minutes left," the Russian said in an awed voice. "Stop talking, for God's sake—I'm trying to contact them now!"

Tension is a curious thing.

Solo had worked hard for it, building an uneasiness in Golgotha and his followers, knowing that when it finally enclosed them in its sweaty palm the odds in favor of him and Kuryakin getting out alive would go up. Golgotha had his dream of world conquest; he had Thrush and its agents to help him. But now these men of flesh and bone stood in a stockpile cemetery in the middle of the night, listening to the roar of a U.S. Army bomber which at any moment might blow them all to bits. Solo knew the human mind. Someone was bound to break. Something *had* to give.

"*Bitte,*" a voice pleaded hoarsely from the ring of guns and lights. "They waste valuable time—"

Shaking with rage, Golgotha spun on the voice.

"Silence!" he screamed. "Who dares question my authority—" For that brief second while his cloaked back was to Solo, Golgotha's body was a barrier against the threat of the sub-machine guns.

Kuryakin spotted the split-second opportunity as soon as Solo did. At the same instant, they moved—Solo leaping for Golgotha, Kuryakin grabbing for the hand grenades taped to his harness straps. A high cry of warning split the night, but there was no time for any of Golgotha's men to dare a shot.

Solo swept Golgotha backward, forcing the trench-knife to the man's neck, digging his knee into the cloaked figure where he thought the small of the back should be. His first intention had been to use Golgotha as a shield for the safe travel of himself and Kuryakin from the cemetery. But now there was no need for that. Golgotha let out a strangled cry of rage. No machine-gun barked and Solo had his sudden, startling answer. They would not shoot if it meant the death of their leader. But more than that, Kuryakin too had free rein.

A metallic hand grenade, looking like a mottled egg, flipped in an arc toward the group behind the lights. Solo bore Golgotha to the ground and burrowed deep. But the man came with him scratching and tearing, his hands like claws.

They found his throat, twisting away from the trench knife as Solo thrust savagely. He had forgotten—the blade clanged tinnily and he cursed himself for not remembering the oddness of this man with the burned, withered body. Some sort of protective chain mesh collar encircled the fiercely-ravaged throat—

And then there was no time to think.

The grenade detonated with a bursting, blinding roar

of metal and fragments. A man screamed hideously before the explosion trailed off into a dying gurgle of sound. A sub-machine gun stuttered now, its coughing noise popping like fireworks across the open air. Kuryakin yelled something. And another grenade echoed the thunder of the first one. Glass shattered and the earth seemed to lift in a soaring gravitational pull that left Solo feeling weak and giddy. Golgotha's lanky, heavy weight pinned him to the ground.

In the darkness, he heard Kuryakin rushing toward them. The Russian was panting. "Napoleon—are you all right—"

And then, the sharp, unmistakable cough of a hand pistol, a single sound, cracked just above Solo and he heard Kuryakin blurt in pain and wonder.

He blundered to his feet, his ears still pounding from the too-close explosion. His eyes made out the shadowy, weaving form of Golgotha heading across the smoking cemetery.

Kuryakin's voice was close to his feet.

"Get him, Napoleon. Don't mind me. Shoulder wound —I'll call the bomber before it's too late—"

Solo hesitated only a second, then set sail across the cemetery, skirting the mangled corpses of Golgotha's hirelings, barely able to make out the bobbing, weaving cloaked figure of the man who had designed a cemetery as a warehouse for a weapon that could enslave the world.

Golgotha was a ghastly shadow dancing past the tombstones of the Orangeberg graveyard.

ORANGEBERG, UNLIMITED

THE TRAIL ended.

Even in the darkness, he had been able to keep Golgotha's shadow in sight. And then, as he stumbled across a sudden dip in the terrain and came up panting, Golgotha was gone. It was as if the mists and the fog had swallowed him alive. Bitterly, Solo searched the grounds. But it was hopeless. Endless rows of tombstones mocked him. Helplessly, he scanned the earth for some clue to the passage of the ghoul. Yet the earth had swallowed him up. Solo knew full well where Golgotha had gone. Underground, to that damn tunnel with the sliding slab doors. But finding it in this darkness without knowing the way would be impossible.

The sighing wind seemed to mock his thoughts. Defeated, he made his weary way back through the maze of grave markers. There was no time to dally. Golgotha could have gone for re-enforcements.

He might be back, loaded for bear.

Overhead, the blast of the bomber echoed across the skies. He hurried back to where he had left Kuryakin. That was the main concern now—that and wiring this deceptive hellspot with the explosives. Golgotha's stockpile had to go.

There was a bitter, acrid odor in the air when he reached the spot where Kuryakin lay. The Russian's pallor was evident, as was the first aid swab planted squarely to his left shoulder. Solo paid a quick visit to the dead minions to make sure no one was stirring. Satisfied, he got back to Kuryakin.

"How's the shoulder?"

"Sulpha and morphine. I'll hold out."

"Good. I lost the Halloween man back there somewhere. Chances are one of the graves is a dummy passageway leading underground, but it would take the night and the day to find it and I wasn't about to play eeny meeny miny mo. Can you navigate?"

"Yes, I think so."

"Did you call the girl friend?"

Kuryakin nodded. "They'll circle for another twenty minutes and pick us up at 2100 precisely. We've got just about time to do what we came to do. I suggest a five minute fuse, just in case."

"Sounds splendid. Come on."

Kuryakin swayed to his feet. "They missed a bet not mining this place."

"Not really. Too risky. Plenty of German boys would find this a nice place to picnic. Besides, Thrush had nothing to worry about. They never could have guessed that Stewart Fromes would pinpoint the spot for us the way he did."

"That's true. Napoleon, let's hurry—before I pass out from loss of blood."

They worked in quick, expert silence for a full fifteen minutes. The nitro jelly, each pound affixed with a blasting cap, was advantageously placed in the northern, southern, eastern and western extremeties of the cemetery. These in turn were cross-wired to the main course of the explosion. Solo strung the wires into a clock device squarely placed in the heart of the cemetery. The jelly by itself would never do the job, but along with it they planted precisely-calculated quantities of the U.N.C.L.E. fire-explosive X-757. Six ounces of it were sufficient to raze a four-story building; a pound of it should raise merry old hell with Orangeberg.

Solo set the clock device, and filled his pockets with samples of the pellets from Wilhelm Vanmeyer's coffin.

"The Old Man would have my hide if I didn't bring him back some souvenirs."

Kuryakin consulted his watch, shaking his head.

"God knows how much of the stuff is here. They may have filled a thousand coffins. And then—" He winced, holding his shoulder.

Solo eyed him.

"You think five minutes is enough time for you, Illya?"

"Try me, Napoleon."

"Five it is, then. Time."

They didn't wait. They fled back to the low wall in the darkness, clambered over and headed for the rendezvous point with the bomber. Even now they could hear the steady symphony of its flight somewhere in the darkness overhead. Solo steadied Kuryakin at one point and led him quickly across the hard ground.

Their boots touched the meadows again. The gloom had dissipated somewhat here in the flatlands. Still, the mists and clouds did not vanish entirely. Both men were concentrating on the cemetery behind them. Suppose something went wrong with the timing device? It had happened before. It could happen again. Nothing, nobody was infallible. And there was always the unpleasant possibility that the mysterious Golgotha had returned to spot their handiwork and had only waited for them to leave to destroy the mechanism.

They stumbled on over the hard ground. Time was passing quickly. Surely the five minutes time allowed for the fuse had passed—

"Napoleon—"

"Don't talk. Walk."

"The plane. There it is—"

Ahead, looming on the lighter patch of ground, was the mammoth bird which had dropped them into Golgotha's graveyard.

The savage backwash of propellors had flattened the blades of grass like a field of rice to be reaped. Solo helped Kuryakin toward the ship, waiting for the sound that did not come.

Would it?

The air door was flung backwards, spilling light onto the darkened field. A helmeted officer stood framed in the entrance, beckoning. Solo saw Jerry Terry poised at his shoulder, peering anxiously into the darkness.

He began to run, pulling Kuryakin with him. The shadow of the ship loomed in his eyes, bigger than his fondest hopes, larger than the wildest dreams of a monster named Golgotha.

"Solo!" Jerry Terry called. "Is that you—"

"Napoleon," Illya Kuryakin's voice came bitterly, close to his ear. "I make out six minutes. Something has gone wrong. We—"

Solo laughed. "I made it seven minutes. I didn't know how much you would slow us up, you lame wolfhound."

"Seven minutes," Kuryakin echoed. "Why you double-crossing—"

The rest of the diatribe was lost in the distant thunderclap of the violent explosion rocking the flatlands behind them. The ground heaved, the earth trembled, the wind increased in fury and velocity. A high keening of destruction filled the shadows of the night.

Orangeberg lit up the sky.

And Jerry Terry fell laughing and sobbing right into Napoleon Solo's outstretched arms.

The bomber crew helping them on board exchanged impressed looks.

"That's it, huh?" a freckle-faced Sergeant asked, poking a thumb in the direction of the blast.

"Yes, that's it," Illya Kuryakin said flatly. But his eyes were shining.

"That's it, all right," Solo agreed, surrounding Jerry Terry's lithe body with his arms. "But it's also the sound of something else."

"What's that?" Sergeant Freckles wanted to know.

Solo stared at him, no longer smiling.

"It's the sound of a man named Stewart Fromes having the very last laugh there is."

Freckles grinned. "That's the best kind of laugh there is."

"Sometimes, fellow. Sometimes."

The air door closed and the bomber rumbled forward, aiming its streamlined nose toward the east. Motors thundered, propellors churned, temporarily drowning out the reverberating destruction behind them. The Orangeberg cemetery was dying noisily.

"Napoleon," Jerry Terry said seriously, "I want to apologize."

"What for?" he asked, still studying the night sky over Orangeberg from the port window.

"I behaved like a kid back there. That Fairmount woman. I'm sorry I acted like a schoolgirl. You did what you had to do."

"Thanks," he said drily. "But you're not a Girl Scout. People die in our business. They have to. Being a woman doesn't change things one way or the other."

"Am I forgiven?"

"Completely," he said, still looking toward Orangeberg. A bright orange flash burst skyward, lighting up the darkness.

"Burn in hell, Golgotha," Napoleon Solo whispered fervently.

ANOTHER SOLO PERFORMANCE

"REALLY, Solo," Partridge protested in a low voice so that no one else standing at the bar of the Paris Overseas Press Club could hear him, "I do think you could fill me in a bit about this Orangeberg thing."

Napoleon Solo shrugged characteristically.

"I thought the AP covered it rather thoroughly."

Partridge made a face. "Oh, yes. Strange explosion in German cemetery. Whole bloody place destroyed. Authorities at a loss and a confounded etcetera. Really, Solo."

"Really nothing, Billy."

"Yes, of course. I suppose you're right. But you chaps in the field always seem to get the best of it. Old I may be and I do have a touch of arthritis in several places but you see, one wants for a little excitement now and

158

then. Keeps the endocrines working properly and all that."

Solo smiled. "I suppose it does, at that. I usually prefer beautiful women, though."

"Like your girlie from Army Intelligence?"

"You're getting warm."

Partridge smiled sourly. "Not as warm as you, I'll wager."

Napoleon Solo slid off his stool. "And here is our beautiful leading lady now."

Coming toward them was the vision who went by the name of Geraldine Terry. She was tall and athletically graceful in a beige woolen sheath dress, her long, copper colored hair neatly swept to one side in a fashionable one-shoulder fall. Her firm, high breasts made more than one man at the bar turn to cast appreciative eyes at her.

"Hello, Miss Terry," Partridge brightened. "Buy you a drink?"

"Thank you, Billy, you may." She smiled at Solo. "Am I late?"

He made a show of consulting his watch.

"Exactly three seconds. I counted." Partridge sniffed the air as if he didn't approve of all this romantic nonsense between fellow agents. Yet, even as he ordered a martini for Miss Terry, he was wistfully approving of her fine figure. Rather lean for his tastes, but then, Americans did tend to starve themselves for their appearance.

"Solo," he began again, manfully.

"Yes, Billy?"

Solo's dark eyes mocked him, waiting. Confound the fellow. He was as tightly buttoned as a cheap ulster.

"Forget it. Passing thought."

"I'll mail you a report, Billy. Scout's honor."

Jerry Terry laughed and speared the olive in her martini.

"What shall we drink to?"

Partridge reached for his glass. "I have one. Let's drink to agents who keep their mouths sealed and don't confide in fellow agents."

"Ouch," said Solo.

They each sipped their drinks. Partridge cocked an eye at Geraldine Terry.

"And you, my girl. Back to the States?"

She looked sober for an instant and then it passed. "Yes, I'm afraid so. I have to check back to the Pentagon by Friday."

"We have two whole days, then," Solo reminded her, staring at her evenly across the rim of his glass. "That can be a lifetime when the people are right."

Before she could answer, a white-jacketed house boy appeared at Partridge's elbow. The Englishman scanned him dourly.

"Well, garçon?"

"Pardon," the Frenchman apologized. "Is this gentleman with you Mr. Napoleon Solo?"

Solo tensed. He suddenly had the old feeling of the world closing in again, enfolding him. Trouble never knew the time of day, the hour or the minute.

"Yes," he said tightly. "I'm Napoleon Solo."

The houseboy smiled. "Phone call, Sir. Long distance. A Mr. Alexander Waverly. He said it was urgent—"

The man from U.N.C.L.E. kissed Jerry Terry on the cheek as he walked swiftly by her to take the call.